Blue Collar Bluff

A Spicetown Mystery

Sheri Richey

Copyright © 2019 Sheri S. Richey. All rights reserved. No part of this book may be reproduced or transmitted in any form or by any means, electronic or mechanical, including photocopying, recording or by an information storage or retrieval system now known or hereto after invented—except by a reviewer who may quote brief passages in a review to be printed in a magazine or newspaper—without permission in writing from the publisher.

For further information, contact the publisher: Amazon Publishing.
The author assumes no responsibility for errors or omissions that are inadvertent or inaccurate. This is a work of fiction and is not intended to reflect actual events or persons.

ISBN: 9781687589620

Cover art by Mariah Sinclair

Spicetown Mysteries

Welcome to Spicetown
A Bell in the Garden
Spilling the Spice
Blue Collar Bluff
A Tough Nut to Crack

Romance by Sheri Richey:

The Eden Hall Series:
Finding Eden
Saving Eden
Healing Eden
Protecting Eden
Completing Eden
∞
Willow Wood

Construction Crew:

Max Alvarez - Electrician

Joe Barney - Carpenter

Cody Beck - Dry wall installer

George Compton - Electrician

Joshua Finley - Carpenter

Ken Hardy - Dry wall installer

Owen Hollingsworth - Carpenter

Henry Knapp - Plumber

Grant LeMasters - Heavy equipment operator

Sammy Lowe - Heavy equipment operator

Donny McBride - Carpenter

Cyrus McDaniels - Carpenter

Cheryl Pittman - Welder

Ralph Rodgers - Plumber

CHAPTER 1

Spicetown Police Chief Conrad Harris yanked open the door of the Fennel Street Bakery and let the aroma clear his cluttered mind. Fretting over travel plans had given him a tension headache, and his departure time was nearing. Coffee and cinnamon rolls were his morning embrace, and he would miss them both. He needed to say goodbye.

"Morning, Mayor," Conrad said as he approached Cora Mae Bingham's table in the middle of the restaurant. Waving to his small morning coffee group at the end of the bar, he scanned Cora's large round table scattered with papers. "Have you decided to move City Hall down here?"

"Good morning, Chief." Cora motioned for him to have a seat. "No official move plans yet, but I like to think of this as my satellite office."

Conrad chuckled as he pulled out a chair.

"The usual, Chief?" The waitress turned Conrad's coffee cup right side up when he nodded. "Coming right up."

"Thanks, Vicki."

"Are you all packed and ready to go?" Cora straightened her papers and tucked her notebook in her bag. "Is Briscoe ready?" The Spicetown City Council had approved funds for Conrad to take his newly acquired shelter dog, Briscoe, to a police training camp in Kentucky.

"Briscoe is always ready. I've got to meet with Wink this morning, and then we'll hit the road."

"Where is Briscoe?"

"I left him at the station. He likes to hang out in dispatch." Conrad nodded his thanks as a waitress handed him a plate with a cinnamon roll on it.

"I'm so glad Shelby introduced you to Briscoe. She's worked at the animal shelter for over ten years, but this is the first time she's ever come to me about a unique dog she found. He must really be something if he stood out that much to her."

"He's pretty special. I doubt he'll have any trouble with this training program. I've got a feeling I'm the one that will flunk."

"Lucky for you, Briscoe is the only one that has to pass a test," Cora said, pushing her plate away. "The insurance company hasn't thought about the dog handler being a city liability yet." Cora Mae chuckled.

"They've got nothing to worry about in Briscoe. He's better behaved than any of my officers." Conrad shook his head and smiled. "Maybe the City Council would like to send Roy off to obedience school next."

"Isn't there a saying about teaching an old dog new tricks?" Cora giggled as she slurped her tea.

"Yeah, he's hopeless." Conrad glanced out the front windows of the bakery and saw a semi-truck with a flat trailer stacked with iron trusses move slowly down Fennel Street. "How's the community center coming along? I haven't been down there lately."

"Oh, it's moving along nicely. We're a little behind, but—"

"We? Are you working down there now, too?" Conrad smiled warily. Cora was prone to over-involve herself in projects.

"I'm just keeping an eye out. I check in once a day or so. I'm not meddling. I'm actually learning a lot, and I enjoy the atmosphere."

"My neighbor, Henry Knapp, is working down there. He said the project manager is a woman." Conrad popped the last bite of his cinnamon roll in his mouth.

"Is that a problem?" Cora's eyebrows arched as she tilted her head in inquiry.

"No. No, not at all. Henry just said he hadn't worked for her before. He knows the site supervisor from some other job but didn't know the new project manager."

"Hmm," Cora huffed in acceptance of Conrad's wiggling out of that conversation. "I've met Henry. He's working with Ralph Rodgers, plumbing out the lobby restrooms. They haven't started building out the front entrance design yet. That's the only big change to the exterior. I'm excited to see how they do that."

"I'm sorry to miss all the excitement," Conrad said. "I'm going to meet with Wink and then hit the road."

"I'm sure Wink is happy to work dayshift for a while. I hear he's courting the new gal at Louise's Beauty Shop. It's difficult to have a dating life if you are working midnights." Cora's sly smile caused Conrad to frown.

"Hopefully, things will be quiet while I'm gone."

"I'm sure," Cora said with a dismissive wave. "You and Briscoe enjoy your stay in Kentucky, and we'll be just fine here. You won't miss a thing."

CHAPTER 2

"You're late."

"And good morning to you too, boss." Owen Hollingsworth stomped his boots to shake off the dust.

Site Supervisor Alan Avery hugged his clipboard to his chest. "I need to see you before you clock out today. Come by my office."

Owen nodded. "Do I need a rep?"

"If a union representative was needed, I would advise you of that. You're up on the southwest corner, second floor, with Barney today."

"Okay." Owen grabbed his hard hat and jogged off.

"Trouble with Owen again?" Erika Johnson asked as she walked up with a stack of notebooks and a pink hard hat in her hands.

"Yeah, he left all his stuff out again last night and he's late today." Turning to go up the stairs of the work trailer, Alan held open the door for Erika.

"What's his excuse this time?" Erika dropped the stack she was carrying on her desk with a thud.

"I don't know. I told him to come by at the end of the day. Barney's been up there waiting on him already, so his lame excuse isn't worth further delays. I'm sure his cat got sick or his brother's half-uncle died. He's always got some excuse he thinks I should care about. He's getting paid well. Why can't he just show up and earn his pay?"

"How many times has he been late?" Erika tried on the pink hard hat and then pulled out a permanent marker to write a name on the inside band.

"I've lost count. He makes it up at the end of the day, but what he doesn't get is he's delaying everyone else. It affects the whole team, and his attitude has damaged this whole project."

"Are you inviting the union?"

"No. It's not worth it to write him up. It's been made clear to me that the company wants him on this job, even if he's a loser."

"I thought I saw the union rep in your office last week. Was that about Owen?"

"You could say that," Alan said, spinning his chair around to face Erika's desk. "He wanted to file a grievance because he didn't have the tools he needed to do his job."

"What? What was he doing?"

"Just normal work, but he left his tools out and somebody stole them. The next morning, he filed the grievance because it is somehow *my* problem that he can't do what he's told and take care of the equipment."

"You're kidding," Erika chuckled. "He's got some nerve."

"I wish I could find the humor. He's filed so many nuisance grievances that he's either trying to waste time with the rep so he doesn't have to work, or he actually thinks he's going to get me fired. I don't know what his motivation is, but he makes this job miserable for everybody."

"I thought he was pretty popular with the guys."

"Some of them act that way, but they do it just to avoid being on his bad side. He has some haters, but most try to keep the peace. Barney is his only real friend, and even he privately complains that Owen slows down the work and messes up. I think everyone would be happier with him gone. I sure would be."

"I can understand that."

"What's the pink hard hat about? Somebody at the lumberyard making a bad joke?" Alan frowned and shook his head.

"No, I went down there to drop off the order sheet for next week and I saw this. I thought it might be nice for the mayor to have her very own special hat." Erika nodded sharply. "I always feel guilty giving her these dirty ones we have sitting around. She's got to go back to work at City Hall."

"Yeah, some of them are filthy."

"Plus, it will make her easier to find. She's always wandering around and popping up in unexpected places."

"She's a hoot. Best teacher I ever had."

Erika's eyes widened. "She was your teacher?"

"Sure was," Alan grinned. "Fifth grade. Taught me fractions!"

"Thank goodness," Erika said with a chuckle.

"Really. She's the reason I loved math. She made it fun. Mrs. B made it cool to be good at it, you know."

"Yeah, I get it. Everybody needs a teacher like that." Erika glanced at the clock on the wall. "It's about time for her to pop in."

"I'm headed upstairs if you're looking for me. Tell Mrs. B I said hey, if I miss her." Alan grabbed his clipboard and pushed open the trailer door.

"Will do," Erika hollered out behind him.

§

"Hey buddy." Conrad rubbed his knuckles between Briscoe's ears when he sat up at straight Conrad's approach. "Everything okay, Georgie?"

"Yeah, Chief. All quiet."

"I need to talk to Wink a minute and then I'm heading out."

"Okay, Chief. Wink's in the break room, I think." Georgia reached out to stroke Briscoe's pointed ear. "You be good at school, little guy." Briscoe's tail wagged in response and he followed Conrad down the hall.

"Hey, Wink," Conrad said as he walked in the break room and sat down.

"Morning, Chief. Are you about ready to go?"

"Yeah, we're going. I left last night's reports with Georgia and posted the updated schedule. There is one thing I failed to mention yesterday."

Wink pulled out a chair at the table and sat down, stirring his coffee.

"That construction project is still going on down at the old popcorn factory."

"Yeah, Chief. We still have it in the nightly patrol pattern and we're keeping an eye on it."

"Good," Conrad said nodding. "The thing is, you might want to stop by there during the day and stroll around a little. The mayor is going down there every day and she's probably a lot more involved than she needs to be."

"She's probably keeping things on schedule," Wink said with a chuckle.

"There was a theft last week, and she's told me there have been a few accidents. She probably doesn't need to be down there, but—"

"That's beside the point," Wink said in understanding. "I'll try and keep an eye out."

"If she needs anything," Conrad said with a raised eyebrow, "I told her to talk to you."

"Sure," Wink said with a shrug.

"A word of caution," Conrad leaned forward on his elbows and searched for a delicate way to convey his concerns. "Maybe I should call it advice."

Wink frowned. "I'm sure it will be okay. I get along just fine with the mayor."

"Yeah. Yeah, I know. If she comes to you with a concern, just roll with it. Don't argue with her or try to talk her out of it. None of that stuff works." Conrad sat back and scrutinized Wink. "Does that make sense? I mean, you can't dismiss her. She'll go forward with or without you and for her own safety, she needs you with her."

"I get it, Chief. You don't want anything to go south. I promise I'll try to keep everything on an even keel until you get back."

"Okay," Conrad shrugged in defeat. He couldn't anticipate what might happen in his absence and he couldn't properly articulate the possibilities. He could only hope everyone was safe and he returned in time for damage control. "I'll see you in a few weeks. Call me anytime you need me."

CHAPTER 3

"Erika," Cora called out as she knocked on the trailer door. "Are you in there?"

"Come on in, Mayor. I'm here."

"Good morning," Cora Mae said as she stepped inside and pulled the trailer door shut behind her. "The weather looks all clear this week. How are you today?"

"I'm great," Erika said, reaching for the hard hat. "I got you something at the lumberyard this morning. I think you need your very own hard hat."

Cora's surprise turned to delight as she reached out to take the hat from Erika's outstretched arms. "Oh, my goodness. You didn't have to do that."

"I know our hats are pretty battered and you needed something special. I can't explain it, but when I saw it, you immediately came to mind. I hope it fits nicely."

Cora put the hat on and laughed as she modeled it. Pink would clash terribly with her copper hair, but the thought charmed her. "Thank you, dear. That was very thoughtful of you."

"You're very welcome."

"So, what's up today? I saw the trusses were delivered earlier." Cora removed the hard hat and took a chair across from Erika.

"They're here, but we aren't ready for them yet. I haven't walked around to check on things today. You're welcome to join me."

"Certainly," Cora said, jumping up from her chair. "Let's go."

Erika led the way outside and Cora followed quickly behind. Now that the second story stairwell had been secured, she hadn't found it difficult to get around the interior, but it was always important to watch her step. Trucks were beeping back up signals and shouting voices were heard left and right. It was the bustling busyness of the work site that Cora enjoyed. The feeling that things were happening all around her every minute. It energized her.

"Henry and Ralph are finishing up the lobby restrooms this week. They've extended it down to that wall," Erika said, pointing to show Cora the full length.

Cora nodded, knowing the plans well. Smiling and waving to Henry and Ralph, she could see the structure beginning to take shape. "When will work begin on the entrance?"

"Not for another week, probably. Alan might have a better idea. It depends on how the framing upstairs is coming. I think he's up there. Let's go check with him."

As Erika scurried up the stairs, Cora stopped halfway up. She looked at the vast emptiness of the large belly of the building. It was just a dark concrete hole right now, but with flooring, paint and lighting, Cora could imagine a beautiful hall to hold holiday events and celebrations. Having an indoor area of this size in Spicetown was going to create endless possibilities. She was anxious for presentation day and had already begun making a list of opening events.

"Mayor?" Erika stopped at the top of the curving steps.

"Yes, dear. I'm coming. I'm just daydreaming." Reaching the top of the steps, Cora heard more voices, but these seemed less instructional and more heated.

"How did this happen? I don't understand how you've stayed in this business so many years when you can't square up a wall. Tear this all down."

"Sounds like Alan is having a little trouble over there," Erika said forcing a grin. "Maybe we should start over on this side. Oh, excuse me, Mayor," Erika said, grimacing as her cell phone rang. "I need to take this."

Cora smiled and nodded but ignored her suggestion to avoid the disagreement and walked toward Alan Avery's voice.

"Rip this out and fix it. We can't keep losing time over your screw ups."

"Good morning, Alan," Cora said, smiling. Alan's face was red, and his blood pressure was probably too high.

"Morning, Mrs. B," Alan said after taking a deep breath. "How are you today?"

"I'm fine. How is everyone today?" Cora looked around the room that would be a small office space on the upper level at the front of the building. "Joe. Owen." Cora nodded to each of them.

"Morning, Mayor. We've got a little hitch here, but we're going to straighten it right out," Joe Barney said with a toothy grin. "Don't you worry."

"I'm not worried at all," Cora said with a wink.

"I'll check back with you before lunch. Mrs. B, we put in one of the new windows on the side this morning. Come take a look." Alan held out his hand to steer Cora across to the other side.

After they were several feet away, Alan hung his head and spoke softly to Cora. "I'm sorry about that, Mrs. B. I just have one guy and I've got to keep an eye on him."

"That's quite all right, Alan. You're just doing your job. I know Joe Barney has worked in construction his whole life. Is he training Owen?"

"Oh, no," Alan said and then chuckled. "That's the part that's driving me crazy. Owen Hollingsworth was his mentor. He's probably mentored half of the guys on this job site."

"Is he the one making mistakes?"

"He is," Alan said shaking his head. "It's not just a mistake here and there. It's a lot of things. I don't want to trouble you with all that, though."

"Being a supervisor is not an easy job, Alan."

"It sure isn't, Mrs. B." Alan chuckled. "It must be a lot like having a room full of fifth graders."

"Not that bad, surely," Cora said, smiling. "At least, I hope not."

§

"Spicetown Police Department. Can I help you?" Georgia Marks said between breaths.

"Georgie? It's Conrad."

"Oh, hey Chief. Are you there yet?"

"No. Just coming up on Lexington now."

"Is everything okay?"

"Sure. I just forgot something I needed to tell Wink. Is he around?" Harold Hobson was Conrad's right-hand officer at the Spicetown PD, but he had been known affectionately as Wink since he was a young man. He had one eye that didn't open all the way and he told everyone it was his good eye. Conrad had never asked him about it.

"Yeah. He's in the break room. You'll have to give me a minute to go get him."

Conrad heard a radio call in the background, and he waited for Georgia to respond and clear the call. "I'm back, Chief. Let me go get him."

"Wait, no. That's okay. You can just tell him to call when he gets back to his desk."

"That's where he's sitting now, the break room. He's not using his desk out here anymore."

"What? Why not?"

"He said there's no privacy out here and until you get back, he's staying in there."

"But there's no intercom in there," Conrad barked as he frowned at the navigation screen in his car. "You can't run back and forth all day. I'll call his cell."

"I think he's on it," Georgia said. "Just a sec."

Conrad waited through another radio call until Georgia was free again.

"I'm back. He's talking on his cell phone, so you'll probably get voice mail. I can go get him."

"This is crazy. There's no phone in there. He can't just camp out in the break room. Why does he need so much privacy?"

"You know, Chief. He wants to talk on the phone without the guys around."

"I don't know. Who is he talking to?"

"You know," Georgia said, urging Conrad to fill in the blanks.

"What? I've been gone all of two hours, and all of a sudden Wink's a recluse?" Conrad gritted his teeth and shook his head. Briscoe cocked one ear up in concern.

"Chief, he's got a new girlfriend. He wants to talk privately."

"He can talk to her when he's off duty. That's ridiculous. Go get him."

"Okay, but you didn't hear that from me," Georgia said as she clicked the phone to hold so she could dash off to the break room again.

"Briscoe, have you ever heard so much nonsense?" Conrad glanced over and thought he caught Briscoe rolling his eyes.

"Okay, Chief. I'm transferring you," Georgia said before switching the call over to Wink's desk.

"Hey, Chief," Officer Hobson said as he leaned back in his desk chair. "Are you there yet?"

"No, I'm still driving. Georgia said you're camped out in the break room. That's the reason I called. I forgot to tell you that you can use my office while I'm gone."

"Oh, wow. That's great. Thanks."

"Don't spend all day chatting up your lady friend, though."

"Ah, no, Chief. I wouldn't do that."

"What's that about, anyway? I didn't know about you dating somebody. Why does everybody else know about this?"

"Because this is one darn nosy town, that's why," Wink said with a snarl. "Sorry, Chief. You know how it is."

"So, who is it? Anybody I know?"

"Mitzi Boyle," Wink said in a hushed tone. "She's a new hairdresser at Louise's Beauty Shop. Just moved here from Paxton."

"So, she's working?"

"Yeah."

"Then she doesn't need to be chatting on the phone all day either," Conrad snapped. "Don't make me sorry I offered."

"I won't, Chief. I appreciate it."

"I'll call you later." Conrad punched the button on the screen to disconnect the call before Wink could respond and looked at Briscoe. "Maybe this trip is a good thing, boy. I need some time away from all of them."

CHAPTER 4

"I'd really prefer it if you didn't chastise the guys right in front of the mayor, Alan." Erika sat down at her desk in the corner of the trailer and Alan Avery spun around in his chair to face her.

"The whole wall has to be torn down, Erika!" Alan blew out the air from his puffed cheeks. "I didn't know Mrs. B was here, and I didn't see her coming. I know it sounded bad, but we've lost a half day of work again. It isn't square. This mess is delaying the welder and we're going to end up paying her wages to wait again because we won't be ready for her."

"I understand you're frustrated."

"Frustrated! He's sabotaging the whole project one stupid move at a time!" Alan slapped his pencil down on the clipboard.

"Alan, it's okay. Owen's not a bad guy. Maybe it wasn't even his fault. Owen has been around for years. Cut him a break. We'll make up the time."

"A break? He's had a break a day since this started. I can't wait for this to be over. I would love it if he just walked off this project tonight and never came back."

"Alan, you can't let this stuff get to you. The contractor isn't upset. They know delays happen. The mayor isn't pushing us either. Just relax."

"I don't understand why nobody seems to be bothered by all this waste. Materials and time. Owen Hollingsworth should not be on this job. Maybe he used to be great, but he's not now. We need to fix what's broken here."

"You need to accept what you cannot fix," Erika said as she pulled out her desk drawer. "Work around him."

"Ugh," Alan said as he spun his chair back around. "People should earn their pay. That's all I'm asking. The guy costs us money the instant he shows up for work late."

"You could write him up."

"I've tried that. The union thinks he's a saint and the contractor caved to the union. I got the message. Hands off Hollingsworth."

"Your face is beet red. You'd think you were footing the bill for this whole project out of your own pocket." Erika laughed.

"I'm trying to do *my* job," Alan said somberly. "I think that includes getting rid of the dead weight. Apparently, I'm unreasonable."

"Oh, Alan, it's not that. It's just—"

"You can mark my word. I'll never take a job with Owen Hollingsworth on board again. Lesson learned."

Cora hovered outside the trailer entrance a few minutes more to make certain their conversation had ended before she stepped up on the metal step to tap on the partially open door.

"Knock, knock." Cora lifted the pink hard hat from her head and fluffed her copper curls.

"Hey, Mrs. B," Alan said as he jumped up to open the door wide.

"Sorry I lost track of you after I took my phone call," Erika said as she stretched out her hand to take the hard hat from Cora.

"That's quite all right, dear. I know my way around pretty well now."

Erika nodded and smiled as she put Cora's pink hard hat on a coat hook by the door. "I'm hanging your hat right here for you."

"Thank you, dear. It was very sweet of you to pick that out for me. I did get a lot of compliments from the other workers. I think they really liked it." Cora reached down to grab her purse that was still perched by the chair. "Maybe it's just because they can see me coming earlier and I won't be able to surprise them." She would find it more challenging to blend in now.

"They love your visits," Alan said chuckling. "And I can use all the help I can get keeping an eye on everybody."

"I know your jobs are not easy," Cora said, slinging her purse strap onto her shoulder. "I'll get out of here and let you get on with your day. Take care."

§

"Morning, Amanda," Cora said as she breezed through the doorway. "Did you think I wasn't coming in today?"

"No, I just thought you were down at the factory." Amanda Morgan, Cora's assistant at City Hall, was already planning Cora's day even before she arrived.

"You have an appointment this morning with Ruth Hollingsworth from the library group, and Shelby Worth called to see if she could stop by. She didn't say why."

"Maybe she just wants to check up on our new police officer dog, Briscoe. I told her the city was going to send him to Kentucky for training, but I haven't talked to her since."

"Was everything okay down at the factory?"

"Yes, I think so. It's an interesting place," Cora said, and then frowned at Amanda. "We need to stop calling it the factory, though. We need for everyone to start thinking of it as the new community center and not the old factory."

"You should have a naming contest." Amanda shrugged. "We could put something in the paper."

"You don't think it should just be the Spicetown Community Center?" Cora straightened her posture and looked off to the corner of the room in thought.

"There's nothing wrong with that. I just thought there are other things we could call it. We could give it a spice name, like the streets in town, or dedicate it to someone historical. It might be fun to see what people come up with. We don't have to use any of their names."

"But we'd have to offer them something. If they submitted a name that we used, they would need to be recognized or win something. Don't you think?"

"I think we could offer a tour of the center before it's open to the public, like a private viewing. That could be the prize. Does the city council have to approve the name?"

"They will think so," Cora said with a fluttering of her eyelashes.

"Then you can blame it on them if none of the names are picked." Amanda opened her word processing software to a press release template and began to type.

"That could work," Cora nodded. "Name your new community center." Cora held out her hands to display an imaginary banner and Amanda quickly typed it as her press release title. "Spicetown City Hall is asking for your help naming the new community center. It can be spicy, clever, historical, reverent, or whimsical. We want to know your thoughts on what a fitting name for the restoration project should be. One that will provide our town with a meeting venue to assist, support, and encourage all the citizens of Spicetown. Please send your ideas to City Hall, PO Box Amanda." Cora giggled at the scowl on Amanda's face.

"Maybe we can use our new email account for this?"

"Ah, that is so futuristic of you." Cora tossed her head back to laugh as she strolled into her office. They had shared many conversations about the limitations email created for the older citizens. Cora didn't want to discourage the use, but she wanted to always offer a traditional path as well. "Use whatever you find works best, dear." Amanda would know that meant both options had to be included.

"Good morning, Miss Morgan." Cora heard a familiar voice and glanced out her doorway to see Ruth Hollingsworth as she stepped from the City Hall lobby over the threshold of Amanda's office door in one large step and straightened her posture. She was an extremely tall, matronly woman who held her chin up to add another inch to her stature and her stern serious demeanor intimidated the college-bound seniors she had taught at Cinnamon High School.

"Good morning, Miss Hollingsworth. It's wonderful to see you again. How have you been?" Amanda gave her a big smile.

"My days pass peacefully, Miss Morgan. Thank you. Is the mayor free to see me now?"

Amanda scurried around her desk to Cora's door to announce her old teacher, but Cora smiled and waved her in the door.

"Come in, Ruth. How are you enjoying retirement?" Cora tried to be extra cheery to balance the dour mood that Ruth conjured by her presence. They were teacher acquaintances, but Cora was elementary school and never measured up to Ruth's view of true education.

"Good morning, Cora. I'm here to speak with you about the possibility of a book sale. As you know, I run the book club for the library and have now volunteered my time to act as President of the Friends of the Spicetown Library Association."

"Yes, I'm aware of your group."

"Well, I wasn't certain. I've never seen you at book club. Are you a reader?"

"Yes, Ruth. I'm an avid reader. I have been all of my life."

"Why have you not joined our group then?" Cora motioned for Ruth to take a seat across from her desk.

"I've been told you limit attendance to those that have a college degree," Cora said with a grimace.

"Of course, but you have that. It doesn't matter when or where you earned that degree."

Cora took her seat and hesitated briefly. "I personally prefer to discuss my reading material with others that enjoy the same genres, regardless of their education level."

"Oh dear," Ruth said with a dismissive wave of her hand. "You would find so much more enrichment among educated minds. It's liberating to explore the interpretations of others."

"I agree that soliciting opinions from others is valuable. I just choose a more diverse path. Now, how can the city help you with your book sale?"

"We have a large collection of donated books, and our storage arrangements are limited. The group is hoping to begin holding an annual sale that will provide funds to purchase new books. We have thought about this for years but coordinating use of the school gym was not working out. Now that this new community center is nearing completion, I would like to know what is involved in securing this facility."

"It's too early for me to provide you with solid instruction. The facility isn't projected to open until October, and the City Council hasn't yet established the usage criterion. I know the plans are to offer it for community use with various fundraisers and celebrations anticipated, but it is too early to enroll. I will let the Council know you are interested, and I'd recommend you watch the newspaper for details. We will ask The Spicetown Star to publish an open invitation to book the center as soon as we can."

"Oh, dear. It is a massive event for us. We are a small group and it will take many hours to catalog and price our holdings. We are interested in holding the event for a full day Saturday and possibly Sunday. Can you at least provide me with an estimate? Could you see availability of a weekend in October?"

"I wouldn't want to mislead you. To be safe, I would suggest you look for a date in mid-January or February, after all the holiday functions conclude. I expect the center to be used heavily in the last quarter of the year for holiday related events. Your sale might be just what this town needs to perk up their winter."

"Hmm." Ruth stood from her chair and cleared her throat in displeasure. "I am disappointed to hear that, but I will let the committee know your thoughts. Thank you for your time."

"You're very welcome, Ruth. Have a good day," Cora called out loudly as Ruth left her office without saying goodbye.

"So, she wants the community center," Amanda said walking through Cora's door. "I wondered why she wanted the appointment. She wouldn't tell me when she called to make it. I'm not important enough to know."

"I'm sure it's not that, dear. She just likes to waft in and out amid a cloud of mystery."

"She's scary," Amanda said with a shudder. "Everyone was always afraid of her when she was a teacher. She's so, so cold and rigid."

"She thinks she's being proper, but I agree. She doesn't come off as being very warm or friendly. She's always been that way, and I don't like the fact that she excludes people from the book club meetings. I've told her that before when she's invited me."

"I didn't realize she did that."

"Oh, yes. It's not just pretentious and snobby. It's downright discriminatory, and I won't be a party to it." Cora bristled and pointed a finger at Amanda. "Her brother is one of the workers at the factory, and he's very pleasant. Owen Hollingsworth. When he introduced himself, I asked him if he was related to Ruth and he told me she was his older sister."

"I don't know him," Amanda said, "But I do know his wife, Bonita. My mom does her hair and she's a very sweet lady."

"Hmm, I wonder if they get invited to book club." Cora huffed as Amanda handed her a draft press release.

"Here's a draft for the newspaper, if you want to take a look. I can try to get it down there before deadline today."

"Mayor. Mayor, are you in there?"

Cora looked around Amanda when she heard Harvey Salzman's voice. "I'm in here, Saucy."

"Oh, Mayor. Did you know there's an ambulance at the old popcorn factory? I just drove by there and it's parked out front with its lights on. Have you heard about it? Is everything okay?" Harvey Salzman was Cora Mae's senior citizen watchdog and he was always quick to report any disturbance.

"No, I didn't know, Saucy, but I'll check on it."

"I hope nobody is badly hurt. Construction sites are dangerous places, you know."

"I know, Saucy. Don't you worry. I'll check on it. Thanks for letting me know."

"Sure thing, Mayor," Saucy said as he turned to leave, nodding a greeting to Amanda.

"I better call Wink and see what's up," Cora said, grabbing her phone as Amanda reached for the handle to pull the door shut behind her.

"Hello, Wink? What's going on at the popcorn factory? Have you heard anything?"

"Morning, Mayor. No, I guess not. Heard about what?"

"There's an ambulance down there now. Did they contact you?"

"No but let me check with Georgia. She might have heard radio traffic. Just a minute."

Cora tapped her fingers on her desk patiently and fought her urge to drive down to the construction site herself.

"Nothing's been reported, but we've got an officer near there, so I'll have him check it out. I'll give you a call back as soon as I have some details."

"Thank you, Wink. I appreciate it." Cora glanced at the time in the corner of her computer monitor. She could wait ten minutes, but if he didn't call back by then, she would have to go down there herself.

CHAPTER 5

"Is everything okay here?" Officer Darren Hudson pushed his squad car door shut and stuck his hands in his pockets.

"There was an accident," Erika Johnson said. "One of our employees had a problem with a saw blade or the guard. I'm not sure of the details yet. We just wanted to get him treated quickly."

"Everybody else okay?" Officer Hudson glanced around to the others in the crowd that were looking on while the emergency medical technicians worked in the back of the ambulance.

"Yes, Officer. Everyone else is okay, but—"

"We're going to take him in," the EMT said to Alan Avery. "He's going to need some stitches."

"Sure. Yeah, you do that." Alan looked around the EMT and into the back of the ambulance. "Donny? Do you want me to call your wife? Tell her to meet you at the hospital?"

"Yeah, Avery," Donny McBride called out. "Just tell her I'll need a ride and it's nothing to worry about. I don't need her to freak out."

"Okay, I understand. Sure thing." Alan waved to Donny just as they shut the ambulance doors.

"I was going to call you," Erika said, looking up at Officer Hudson. "I do have another theft I need to report."

"Sure thing," Hudson said. "Just let me call this in and then I can take your report."

Officer Hudson returned to his car and Erika turned to Alan.

"Did Sammy tell you that the belt sander is missing?"

"No," Alan said with a jerk of his head. "I haven't seen him since early this morning, though."

"He said it wasn't locked up and he's walked the whole top floor. He can't find it anywhere."

"Who used it last? Who signed it out yesterday?" Alan dropped his chin and peered at Erika.

"I haven't had time to check on that yet."

"Hmm," Alan said with a frown. "I'll go take a look."

§

"Mayor?"

"Yes, Wink? Did you find out what was going on down there?" Cora switched her phone to the other hand and looked at her clock. Eight minutes was pretty good.

"Yeah, seems one of the workers got cut with a saw blade. Just an accident."

"They seem to have these frequently, and I'm a little concerned. I understand it's a dangerous profession, but I still feel these events are happening too often. Who was hurt?"

"Donald McBride," Wink said.

"Oh, Donny. Is he going to be okay?"

"Yes, ma'am. They said he'd probably need stitches, but nothing serious."

"Oh, that's a relief."

"They've had another theft, though. Hudson is taking the report now."

"Goodness!" Cora said. "That's another thing happening at an alarming rate. Is this normal, Wink? I don't have much experience with construction sites, but do people steal from them all the time?"

"Well, it happens, but it's usually materials that are stolen because there's no way to lock them up. Tools are usually kept track of pretty close. You sign them in and out. They aren't left out overnight. I think they just need a stricter control over them. We're patrolling the place every night."

"I'm surprised. I wouldn't think Alan or Erika would be careless. Have any of your officers seen anyone around the work site at night?"

"No. No reports of any mischief. I'll have them double patrols, though. Maybe I should go down there and talk with them about their security."

"I think they need all the help they can get, Wink. You should stop by and look around the place. It's very interesting, and they are making progress despite all the problems. I check in with them every morning."

"I'll see what I can do, Mayor."

§

"Hi, Mom," Amanda said as she walked in the door of Louise's Beauty Shop.

"Hey, kiddo. What brings you by?"

"I had to run a press release over to the newspaper office, so I was passing by."

"Checking up on me?" Louise Morgan laughed, and Amanda nodded. "Have you met Mitzi Boyle? She's my newest stylist."

"I haven't. It's nice to meet you, Mitzi."

"Hi there," Mitzi said, wiggling the fingers of her free hand as she held her customer's wet hair with the other.

"So, how is the new romance coming along?" Louise Morgan wrapped the freshly cleaned combs in a towel to dab them dry and smiled at Mitzi Boyle.

"You have a new romance?" Claudia Spiller said as she locked eyes with Mitzi in the mirror. "You just moved to town! Who is it? Anybody I know?"

"She's been seeing our Officer Hobson," Louise said with a wink to Amanda. They had discussed this over dinner a few nights before.

"Wink!" Claudia was trying to hold her head straight while Mitzi trimmed her hair, but her eyes darted around in the mirror.

"His real name is Harold." Mitzi smiled. "We've gone out a few times, and I like him."

"You know he's in charge right now?" Louise shared a secret smile with Amanda. "The Chief's out of town and he put Wink in charge."

"Yeah and I thought it was going to be great for him to be on day shift for a while so we could go out on the weekends, but it sounds like he's too busy for that. He's always worked weekends, so we have to go out during the week."

"Too busy?" Louise looked at Amanda. "Is something exciting going on in Spicetown?"

"I don't know," Amanda shrugged.

"I tried to call him this morning during my break, but he said he couldn't talk." Mitzi gave Claudia a pouting face in the mirror and they smiled.

"There was an accident down at the construction site this morning. That was probably what was going on, and he had to check on it." Amanda regretted her words as soon as she saw her mother's eyebrows shoot up.

"An accident? Who was hurt?" Louise tossed the clean combs in the stand at her station.

"Oh, I don't know. Saucy just came by and said he saw an ambulance down there. The mayor was going to call and find out, but then I left to run to The Star to drop off the press release."

"Mitzi, you need to try and call Wink again. See if you can find out who was hurt."

Amanda sighed heavily and touched her mother's arm. "I'm going out to dinner tonight, so don't wait for me. I've got to get back to City Hall."

"Okay, dear. Have a good time," Louise said as Amanda rushed out the salon door, wishing she hadn't contributed to the gossip circle that kept her mother's business thriving.

§

"Maybe I need to call the boss and tell her we need to hire night security. Something strange is going on around here," Erika said to Alan after Officer Hudson left the office trailer.

"What we need to do is get rid of Owen Hollingsworth. You know, we've never had problems like this before. All these thefts have been of tools that Owen checked out without returning. He denies it, but his name is on the sign out sheet every time."

"I'm surprised that the union isn't upset about it," Erika said flipping through pages on a clipboard. "They paid for that belt sander."

"They always stick up for Owen. The union says he couldn't have done it. It makes no sense to me. They're the ones losing money here."

"Yeah, but we're losing time. We have to keep waiting on replacement tools. The accidents don't make sense, either."

"I asked Donny and he said the guard wasn't on," Alan said, frowning. "I don't think the blade was engaged and he may have turned it on before he checked, but Donny isn't careless."

"It's like the loose flooring when Henry got hurt. I don't know how that happened. It had been secure earlier because I'd walked on it. These accidents are weird."

"I'm going to call the union and tell them about the missing sander and Donny's accident." Alan spun around in his chair to face his desk. "I'm going to have to talk to Owen about this, too."

"I'll call and give the contractor an update. This project is never going to be done if all this stuff doesn't stop soon."

§

"Hey, Barney," Owen Hollingsworth said as he brushed sawdust from his pants. "I've got to go see Avery again, so I'm shutting down early. Can you wrap this up?"

"Sure, Owen. What's Avery want?" Joe Barney tossed some small wood shims into a scrap pile in the middle of the room they had been trimming out.

"Who knows. Same stuff as always. He probably thinks I'm the reason Donny got hurt. He thinks everything is my fault."

"Sorry. I know he's been on you a lot since this job started."

"Yeah, it's okay. I get to quit early every day. If he wants to waste time dumping his problems on me, that's his choice."

"You should call the union."

"They've been here but he didn't say I needed them today. He probably just wants to preach at me about something. I need to get to work earlier. I need to be more careful with the tools. I need to be respectful of my coworkers. I need to eat more vegetables." Owen tossed his head back and laughed. "He's become my mama! I couldn't never make her happy, either."

"I've worked for Avery before, when he was down at the county water plant, and he was a decent boss then. I don't know what's made him act this way. Maybe he just doesn't like you, man."

"What's not to like?" Owen lifted his hard hat and held his arms out wide with a smile. "Everybody loves Owen!"

Barney chuckled and shook his head. "Maybe you could make friends with that project manager girl. She could get Avery off your back."

"I tried that. I gave her the Owen charm, and she almost bit my head off. She's pretty cold and got a mean streak." Owen sneered and put his hard hat back on. "You know her boss is a woman, too."

"What?" Barney said looking over his shoulder in surprise. "I thought Roger was running the company."

"Nope," Owen said. "Some woman is in charge now."

"Oh, well there you go."

"Nagged at home and at work!" Owen chuckled as he walked toward the stairs. "See you Monday."

"Wait. Don't forget Sammy's tonight," Joe Barney called out. "The game starts at seven o'clock."

"Hey, I can't," Owen said walking backwards. "Demolition derby is tonight."

"Come by after. We'll still be at it. I may have lost all my money by the time you get there and you can take my spot."

Owen nodded and waved as he headed down the steps to the main floor.

CHAPTER 6

"Hi, Connie," Cora said when she grabbed her ringing phone from her desk. "Are you all checked in and ready for the training assessment?"

"We checked in at the hotel first and just finished a tour of the training site. We're sitting in the bleachers now, watching another class. They have a big show ring in the facility where they run training exercises. The dogs out there now are drug sniffing. It's a professional set up."

"Sounds very interesting," Cora said. "Shelby Worth from the animal shelter said it was supposed to be one of the best police dog schools around. I just wish we could afford all the bells and whistles."

"I think he'll do okay with basic obedience. As long as I'm sure I can control him when we're out on a call, I think just his presence will make a difference."

"He does have an intimidating look about him." Cora smiled. Briscoe was not a dog you reached out to pet without thinking first. He had a serious gaze and a composed but suspicious manner that sent a signal at first glance that he would let you know if he decided to be your friend. He had trusted Conrad right away.

"And he can run faster than I can," Conrad said with a chuckle. "He's watching this training pretty seriously, though. I think he's excited to be here. He seems to know this is all about him."

"Briscoe may just ace the entry exam and you'll be back by the end of the week."

"He may. So far, he seems to understand everything I ask of him. I wish we knew what his back story was, where he came from."

"Shelby is trying to talk me into adopting now, but I don't think Marmalade will approve of that."

"I don't know if Briscoe is cat friendly or not, but I need to find out. When I get back, I could bring him by and we could ask Marmalade."

"You're not using my cat as a guinea pig," Cora said straightening her back. "You need to run that test somewhere else."

Conrad laughed. "I'll be sure and tell him to behave. With this new training, that should be all that I need to do."

"Hmm," Cora said.

"What's going on in Spicetown? I tried to call Wink, but it went to voice mail."

"Well, there was another accident at the construction site, and they took Donny McBride to the hospital for stitches. Wink also told me that they reported another tool theft today. I'm going to go down there later and get firsthand information, but I'm concerned about security over the weekend. Wink said he'd double the patrol around it."

"The construction company could hire some security."

"Yes, I'm going to mention that to Erika when I see her," Cora said. "How's the hotel?"

"It's better than the animal shelter, so Briscoe is happy. We'll survive."

"Amanda was worried about it not being very nice. Not too many people wanted to rent a room to Briscoe. She had a hard time finding something close to the facility."

"Blatant discrimination," Conrad huffed. "He doesn't take it personally, though."

"Well, you boys have fun over there, and stay out of trouble."

"I should remind you of the same," Conrad said. "Let Wink keep an eye on the construction. You just handle the mayoring."

Cora just laughed because she wasn't making any promises.

§

"Hey, Owen," Alan Avery said when Owen Hollingsworth entered the work trailer. He wasn't even on time for this meeting. "Have a seat."

"What's up, boss?"

"Just need to check in with you on a few things. You were late this morning again." Alan glanced down at his list of problems.

"I know, but the wife, she held me up. She's not feeling well, and I'm worried about her."

"I'm sorry to hear that. I didn't know," Alan said. "Do you need some time off?" Alan secretly crossed his fingers under the desk.

"Nah, she's been seeing doctors, but some mornings are just harder than others."

"Well, if you need time off, you just need to let me know. We can always work something out."

"Appreciate that."

"There are another couple of things I needed to run by you," Alan said as he reached for the clipboard on the side of his desk. "Do you see this entry?"

Owen glanced down at the tool sign out sheet.

"There," Alan said pointing his finger. "It shows you signed out a belt sander a few days ago. Do you remember doing that?"

"That wasn't me," Owen said, leaning back in his chair. "I know it's my name, but that's not my writing. I told you that last time. I see what it says, but somebody else is putting my name down."

"Yes, you said that last time. So, you haven't used the belt sander?"

"I've used it. Me and Barney had it on the second floor yesterday, but I don't know who checked it out. He had it before I even got up there."

"Okay," Alan sighed. "Where were you Tuesday morning at 7:28?

"I don't know. Was I even here yet? I don't remember Tuesday, but you can check the timecards."

"I'll do that." Alan sat back in his chair as Owen stood to leave.

"Have you heard anything about Donny? Is he okay?"

"He got a few stitches and it looks like he'll need some time off. Were you there when he got hurt?"

"No, but I heard him yell. The saw didn't sound right, though. He was down on the east side of the second floor. Finley was with him and Beck was coming up the stairs. He heard it, too."

"What did it sound like?"

"The motor sound was weird. He turned it on and yelled before switching it off. It made a sputtering noise. I guess it was faulty or something. Finley might have seen it."

"I'll check with him. Thanks."

"See you Monday," Owen said as he left the trailer and slammed the door.

Yippee. Alan scowled as Erika yanked open the door.

"I saw Owen leaving. Did you find out anything?"

"Just that he didn't do it. That's always his line." Alan tossed his pen on the desk. "At least this meeting was civil. He wasn't yelling and accusing me of targeting him or any of that nonsense. Maybe he just saves that show for the union when they're here."

"That's progress, I guess." Erika shrugged before falling into her desk chair. "I talked to the company, and they don't want to pay for extra night security. We're supposed to walk the area at the end of each day, though, and make sure everything is secure before we leave."

"Let's not hold the employees responsible for anything. Let's just add one more item to management's to-do list." Alan groaned.

"Did you talk to Owen about the wall he had to tear out?"

"No. I would have to invite the union for that and frankly, it isn't worth it. The company won't let me get rid of him, so why should I bother documenting anything? The union gets upset and everyone's mad at me. I give up."

"It will at least explain the extra time if we don't make the contract," Erika said.

"I've got it documented in my notes. I'm just not going to bother trying to write him up. If the company doesn't mind pouring money down the drain with employees like that, why should I?"

CHAPTER 7

"Don't look now," Amanda whispered, leaning forward with her elbows on the table at the Old Thyme Italian Restaurant. "Our Acting Chief of Police just came in the door." Amanda blushed as her boyfriend, Bryan Stotlar, tried to look sideways without turning his head.

"Who's he with?"

"That's Mitzi Boyle. She's a new hairdresser at my mom's shop. She just moved here a few months ago."

"So old Wink still has some moves?" Bryan chuckled.

"Apparently so."

"Chief Harris is out of town?"

"Yeah, he took his dog to that training school in Kentucky, so Wink is in charge. My mom told me she was dating Wink, but I hadn't run into them anywhere. I just met her this morning. I stopped by the shop when I was walking back to City Hall from the newspaper office."

"The article about naming the old popcorn factory?"

"Yeah. Have you got any ideas?"

Bryan stared at his water glass on the table. "You know I'm not creative. I can't think of anything."

"I don't think it'll matter what we call it. Everybody around here is going to call it the old popcorn factory for at least twenty years," Amanda said as Bryan nodded.

"True. They still call the Wasabi Women Dance Club the old drive-in, and the drive-in theater has been gone since I was a kid."

"Hi, Amanda." Mitzi Boyle smiled down at Amanda as she approached their table at the Old Thyme Italian Restaurant.

"Hi, Mitzi," Amanda said as Mitzi glanced at Bryan. "This is Bryan Stotlar. He owns Stotlar Nursery north of town. Bryan, this is Mitzi Boyle. She works with my mom."

"Nice to meet you," Bryan said, extending his hand.

"I've heard all about you," Mitzi beamed.

"I'm sure you've heard a lot of things working at the beauty shop. It's a hub for town gossip." Amanda's jaw clenched.

Mitzi nodded. "Be sure and tell your mom when you see her that it was Donny McBride that was hurt today at the construction site. He's going to be okay, though. He just got some stitches."

"Knowing my mom, she probably already knows that." Amanda felt Bryan's foot nudge her under the table.

"Have a good evening, you two. It was nice to meet you, Bryan." Mitzi scrunched up her shoulders and gave Bryan a wink as she walked away from their table.

"You, too," Bryan said as Amanda took a deep breath.

"Somebody was hurt today?" Bryan frowned and dropped his head down to catch Amanda's eye.

"Yeah. They called an ambulance and Saucy saw it. He came in to tell the mayor about it."

"So, you already know it was Donny McBride?"

"Yes, but I'm not going to feed information to my mother, and she knows better than to ask me about it."

"I don't think she'll be needing to do that anymore," Bryan said as he glanced over at Wink's table. Mitzi was returning and Wink jumped up to pull out her chair for her. "Your mom has a new source now."

Amanda groaned.

§

"Hey, Chief. How are things in Kentucky?" Officer Sam Crawford leaned back in his chair in the Spicetown Police Department dispatch room and stretched out his legs. "Everything is quiet here so far."

"Glad to hear it. Sammy, do you know where Wink is? I tried his cell phone, but it went to voice mail."

"I think he's at dinner, Chief. Is there something I can do for you?"

"No, I just wanted to check in with him. I heard there was a theft and an accident at the old popcorn factory today. I just wanted to see if Wink found out anything."

"Not that I'm aware of, but I just came on duty at four o'clock. I saw the reports, but Georgie didn't say anything had changed. Wink doubled patrol over there."

"I thought maybe the construction company would add some security out there." If Cora asked for something, she usually got it.

"Not that I've heard about."

"I left Wink a voice mail. I'll let you go." Conrad heard a radio call in the background.

"Thanks, Chief. Have a good time."

Conrad huffed into the disconnected phone. There was no way to have fun sitting in a dismal hotel room with a dog. Clicking the remote control to turn on the television, Conrad sat back on the bed and stretch out his legs. "Come on, Briscoe. You can come up here and we'll see what's on TV." Patting the bed beside him, Briscoe leaped up and made himself comfortable. Flipping through the channels, he turned on the news and grabbed his phone. "Let's check in with Cora and see what she's up to."

"Hey, Connie."

"Cora. I can't seem to reach Wink. Did you learn anything more about the situation at the construction site today?"

"No, I got tied up at work. I had planned to stop in before Erika left, but I couldn't make it. I'm out here now looking around—"

"You're at the construction site now?"

"Yes. I was driving by and thought I saw headlights around back, but it was just someone turning around, I think. There aren't any cars here—"

"You don't need to be out there in the dark." Conrad ran his hand over his spiked crew cut hair and sat forward. Briscoe lifted an eyebrow in concern.

"It's just starting to get dark. It's well lit. I don't know—."

"Cora, let patrol take care of it. It's not safe out there, especially with no one around."

"Connie, I'm fine. Did you have a nice dinner? I haven't even been home yet."

"I drove through some fast food place. I can't go anywhere because no one will let Briscoe in. He got a nice run at the facility today once the classes were over, so at least I didn't have to spend all night walking him. It's easier at home where he can run free in the fenced backyard."

"I know you both would rather be home," Cora said. "It's cooling off here, but, wait... I think I hear something clinking. Upstairs on the second floor—"

"Cora, where are you? Don't go up there," Conrad sat up straight and Briscoe was poised to bolt as well.

"I'm on the sidewalk. Wait," Cora said and paused.

Conrad reached for the hotel phone on the table and read the instructions to get an outside line. "Get back in your car."

"Maybe it's nothing."

"I'm going to call and send a car over. You need to get back in your car. Where are you?" Conrad fumbled with the hotel phone and dialed out.

"I'm just out front on the sidewalk. I'm not inside. It's nothing."

"Sammy, send a car over to the popcorn factory," Conrad said holding a phone to each ear and not waiting for Sammy's response. "Cora, get back in your car. Tabor or somebody will be right there. Don't go in—"

"It's nothing, Conrad. I don't hear anything now. There aren't any cars here."

"Burglars don't park out front, Cora."

"Chief? Tabor's on his way." Sammy said, and Conrad heard radio traffic in the background, but didn't respond.

"Yes, I hear it again," Cora said as Conrad looked at the clock. "Oh! Could you hear that? A metal sound like something was dropped."

"Are you in the car? Turn your car on and lock the door."

"I'm going, but—"

"I don't hear the car." Conrad said with a controlled frustration. "Sammy, where is Tabor?"

Conrad heard Cora's seatbelt reminder dinging in the background as Sammy responded. "En route, Chief."

"Cora, roll your window up."

"I can't hear that way, Conrad. Relax. If someone is up there, I've probably scared them off already."

"That's—"

"Could you hear that?" Cora said in a hushed tone. "Somebody's talking up there and they dropped something. I think they're arguing. Oh! A loud boom sound. They're fighting or they threw something. I don't know."

"Sammy, there are people on the second floor," Conrad said into the hotel phone. "The mayor is out there in her car. You might want to send back-up."

"Sure, Chief. Asher's out at the Wasabi—"

"What's he doing there?" Conrad barked at Sammy. "Never mind."

"What?" Cora said in Conrad's other ear.

"Nothing. Tabor will be there in a minute. I can tell him what's going on. You should go on home."

"I'll stay in the car and wait for Eugene. Everything is quiet now. Maybe I'll drive around to the back—"

"No, just—"

"Oh, there he is. I see Eugene. I'll call you back, Connie."

Conrad fumed when Cora disconnected the line and he yelled at Sammy unnecessarily. "Where is Wink?"

"Georgie told me he was going to dinner at Old Thyme Italian. He wasn't here when I came on."

"Okay, sorry. I'm a little frustrated. Look, the mayor is out there snooping around the construction site and she doesn't need to be out there alone. She heard voices on the second floor, sounded like they dropped something, some metal clinking, more than one person up there."

"Asher is on his way. He was handling a disturbance call but—"

"Tell him to make sure the mayor gets home safely."

"Will do, Chief."

"Thanks, Sammy." Conrad hung up the hotel phone and tapped Wink's cell phone number, stored in his favorites.

"Wink's getting one more chance," Conrad said to Briscoe, who had relaxed his shoulders and lowered his head. "He better answer his phone."

Conrad leaned back against the pillows again but was disappointed when his call went immediately to voice mail. Disconnecting the call, he scrolled through his contacts until he found the number for the restaurant. It was one of his frequently called numbers when he worked late and needed a carry-out dinner.

"Hey, Jo Anne. It's Conrad Harris."

"Oh! Hi, Chief. What can I get you tonight?"

"Not ordering tonight. Just looking for Wink. Is he there?"

"Oh, Officer Hobson? I've been back in the kitchen. Let me look out front."

Conrad heard the clatter of dishes and voices barking orders. Friday nights were a busy time for the Old Thyme Italian Restaurant.

"Yeah, Chief," Jo Anne said returning to the phone. "He's here. You want to hold, and I'll go get him?"

"No, that's okay," Conrad said. "If you would, just tell him to step outside and give me a call. I think his cell is turned off."

"Gotcha, Chief."

§

"Evening, Mayor." Officer Tabor had parked on the street in front of Cora's car and walked back to her car.

"Hello, Eugene. I'm sorry to drag you out here, but I thought I saw a car pull out of the back side of the parking lot, so I stopped and got out of my car. Then I heard voices and noises upstairs. I think someone might be up there on the second floor," Cora said pointing to the west side of the building. "I haven't seen any lights, but I heard clanging sounds, scuffling, and a really loud boom."

"There have been some thefts out here. Let me check on it. You can go on home now, ma'am, and thanks for letting us know." Tabor touched the bill of his Spicetown Police ball cap in a mock salute.

"I'll just wait here in my car," Cora said. "Unless you'd like me to drive around the building and see if I see anything."

"No, ma'am. That's not necessary. Officer Asher is on his way. I'd feel better if you were safe at home."

"Well, don't let me delay you. Thank you for coming."

"Yes, ma'am," Tabor said as he turned to enter the building.

Because of the demolition required at the main entrance, there was only a sheet of plywood covering what would eventually be the door and Cora watched as Officer Tabor worked it free to slide it aside. She could see his flashlight beam bounce around the second-floor room and heard some shuffling noises just as Officer Asher's car pulled up. Glancing down at her phone, she ignored a text from Conrad asking if she was home yet and turned off her car so she could hear better once Officer Asher entered the building.

§

"Hey, Chief. Sorry, I didn't know you were trying to get a hold of me."

"Not just me," Conrad said. "Everybody!"

"I didn't know," Wink said defensively. "What's going on?"

"You couldn't possibly know what's going on when you're out running around with your cell phone turned off. I know more about what's going on right now than you do and I'm over a hundred miles away. Maybe I didn't explain my job properly. Maybe I didn't spell it all out for you like I should have. Silly me, I thought you knew what I did and could step right into my job while I was gone. Have you ever tried to reach me and found my phone turned off?"

"No, Chief. I—"

"No, because being Chief of Police means you're responsible for the entire police department day and night. It means the safety of the town counts on you doing the right thing at the right time. You can't do that if you don't know what's going on, and you can't know what's going on with your cell phone turned off!"

"Sorry, Chief. I didn't even realize it. I told Georgie where I was going and I'm just—"

"I know what you're doing. Probably everybody in Spicetown knows what you're doing, and you're entitled to a private life, but you can't have one until I get back!"

"Yes, sir. I'm sorry, Chief. I didn't think—"

"That's stating the obvious." Conrad blew air from his puffed cheeks. "When I get back, you'll have off duty time. Then you can take this woman out of town to eat dinner without the whole town watching you. But right now," Conrad swallowed loudly. "Right now, you are Acting Police Chief. So, act like it!"

"I will, Chief."

"Look, there's something going on down at the construction site. Cora was down there snooping around, and she heard voices, heard noises. Tabor is probably there by now and Asher was going to join him to look around. You need to know that. You need to know what's going on."

"I'll go down there right now, Chief."

"If you find the mayor still hanging around, do what you can to see her home."

"I will. Right now."

Conrad disconnected the call and told himself that throwing the phone at the wall was not productive. Briscoe raised his head up and made a high-pitched whine as if asking what they should do next and Conrad reached out for him.

"It's okay, buddy. It's just tough being away from home. We need to get back there as soon as we can, so you've got to be on your game tomorrow. Can you do that for me?"

Briscoe leaned into Conrad's chest and Conrad put his phone in his lap to wait for Cora to respond to his text.

CHAPTER 8

"Hey, there he is," Max Alvarez called out from the kitchen when Joshua Finley walked into Sammy Lowe's house. "Where have you been? I've almost lost all my paycheck!" Max laughed and offered Josh a drink.

"Double booked!" Josh laughed as he walked around the table to peek over George Compton's shoulder to see what he held in his hand. The bid was getting high and only George and Ralph Rodgers were still throwing chips on the pile in the middle of the table.

"No peeking!" George barked and held his cards close to his chest as Josh chuckled. Ralph frowned and ignored all the banter as he tried to decide on his next bid.

"Out with the ladies?" Max asked Josh with a wink.

"It's Friday night. I'm a single man. I have plans that you old married men can't imagine."

"You tell him." Joe Barney, the only other single man in the group, pointed a finger at Josh. "These old guys can't remember."

"Where's Owen?" Sammy Lowe asked Barney as he opened another bag of chips and cleaned up around the table. He tried to keep the poker night mess to a minimum, so his wife didn't get mad when she got home. "I thought he would come with you."

"I think he was going to the demolition derby tonight. I told him to come by after, if it wasn't too late."

"Henry and I were out there earlier, but I didn't see him," Max said. "Henry, did you see Owen at the derby?"

Henry Knapp reached over and grabbed a taco chip. "Nope. Was he there?"

"He was probably working in a pit crew." Barney grabbed a paper plate and begin filling it with chips. "He likes to do that. He's always buying up parts and working on those cars."

"I may not have seen him then," Max said. "It was over at eight o'clock."

"You got here after eight o'clock and you've almost lost your paycheck?" Josh Finley shook his head in disbelief and Barney laughed.

"He throws it all in there too quick," Barney said.

"I know. I bet too much," Max laughed. "Or maybe I just need a bigger paycheck."

"Go big or go home," Henry said opening the refrigerator. "That's what they say."

"Straight flush," Ralph Rodgers said as George Compton slapped his four of a kind on the table.

"What have you got to eat, Sammy?" George said leaning back in his chair. "I'm going to need a free dinner after that hand."

§

After running some Saturday morning errands, Amanda slipped in the kitchen door, relieved to have returned before it rained.

"Would you like some lunch, honey?" Louise Morgan bustled around the kitchen as Amanda walked in. "Your dad should be home soon and I'm heating up some bread. We're going to have the chicken pot pie soup."

"Sounds good. It looks dreary out there," Amanda said, peeking out the dining room window at the overcast sky. "No sun today."

"I know," Louise said snapping the oven door shut. "It's supposed to rain later and get cooler."

"How was work this morning?" Amanda reached in the cabinet for soup bowls. Louise always opened the beauty shop on Saturday mornings, but they closed at noon.

"Well," Louise said glancing over her shoulder to smile at Amanda. "I got to hear all about Mitzi's date last night."

Amanda had hoped her mother would accept the question as rhetorical and just say her day had gone well. "I saw her last night."

"She told me she met Bryan," Louise said with a shake of her head. "Apparently Officer Hobson ran out on her."

"He was there. I saw them both come in the restaurant."

"Oh, he picked her up and they went, but it was worse than being stood up." Louise turned her back to stir the soup on the stove top.

Amanda frowned. "Why? It isn't working out?"

"He left her there." Louise looked over her shoulder at Amanda and raised her eyebrows. "Didn't you notice?"

"No. She came over to our table and said hello. I introduced her to Bryan, but Officer Hobson wasn't with her. I didn't see them again."

"He left before they even ordered! She is not happy with him." Louise peeked out the window over the kitchen sink. "I think your dad just drove up. Anyway, I tried to tell her that she'd have to get used to that sort of thing. That's what happens when you date a cop. She said it had something to do with the mayor and that construction site. You'll probably hear about it Monday."

Amanda knew her mother was hoping she would bring home a report, but the beauty shop circuit usually heard things before Amanda did. "He is in charge right now. You know the Chief is out of town. It won't always be like that."

"No, she's usually complaining about his schedule. He works nights all the time. Everything has to be scheduled around him and Mitzi seems to want to be the center of attention. I think the only reason she went out with him is because he's a cop. She wants all the town scoop. It might be for protection, too."

"Protection from what?" Amanda blurted out before she thought about her words. She was becoming her mother.

"She had some bad situation in Paxton. She's never really explained it, but it had something to do with the guy she dated over there. I don't know if he treated her badly or what, but that's why she moved."

"Well, it's good that she got away from it," Amanda said as the back door opened. "Hi, Dad."

"Hey, pumpkin," Hymie Morgan said as he slipped off his jacket. "It smells good in here. The wind is kicking up out there. I think it's going to storm."

"A good day to stay home," Louise said as she pulled the warm bread from the oven. "Have a seat. Lunch is ready."

Hymie Morgan sat down at the kitchen table and Amanda carried steaming bowls of chicken pot pie soup to the table.

"I was just telling Amanda that Wink Hobson walked out on Mitzi Boyle last night when they were on their date. He took her to dinner at Old Thyme Italian Restaurant and left before they even ordered." Louise sat a basket of warm bread on the table and poured iced tea into glasses that Amanda had lined up on the counter.

"I'm sure he had official business," Hymie said, leaning into the aroma of the soup and inhaling.

"I don't even know how she got home. I'm sure he drove them there. He could have at least taken care of that." Louise passed out the drinks and took a seat.

"If I'd have known, she could have come to our table," Amanda said and then explained to her father. "Bryan and I were in there at the same time. She said hello to us. I didn't realize Officer Hobson had to leave."

"Cora Mae is always yanking the Chief around. I guess since he's out of town, she's going to pull Wink everywhere. I don't know why she gets herself involved in police things all the time."

"She's the mayor, mom. Everything going on in this town is her responsibility." Amanda hoped her stern response let her mother know that this line of discussion was closed.

"I don't think Mitzi can deal with that, with Wink just running off without notice." Louise shook her head as she buttered her bread.

"Public service is a demanding occupation. They've both got to do what they need to do. You either accept it or you don't." Silence followed Hymie's declaration and Amanda reminded herself once again that idle conversations with her mother were risky. It had taken years for their relationship to mend from her teenage years and she didn't want to disrupt that harmony.

§

"Afternoon, Chief. It's Wink. Are you busy?"

"No, not a bit. I'm just sitting here watching Briscoe horse around. What's up?"

"I just got a call from Bonita Hollingsworth. Do you know her?"

"No, the name doesn't ring a bell."

"She said her husband didn't come home from work Friday and she wants to file a missing person report. His name is Owen Hollingsworth."

"I've met him once down at the construction site. The mayor introduced me to several of the guys. She knows them all."

"I'm told he's never gone missing before. I mean, he's not one to go off for a few days or anything. Nothing in the files on either of them. She said he went to work Friday morning at the old popcorn factory and never came home. She thought at first he was out with the guys, but she talked to his buddy, Joe Barney. All the guys were together Friday night and Owen didn't show."

"Was he at work Friday?"

"Apparently," Wink said. "Barney told her that he invited him to poker night at Sammy Lowe's house, but he said he was going to the demolition derby."

"Were they fighting?"

"She said everything was fine. No trouble. Just a normal day."

"Why didn't she report it Friday night?"

"Said she thought she had to wait 48 hours. She's checked around with friends and such, though."

"There's no way to know if he went to the derby or not. There were probably a few hundred people there. You might want to call Joe Barney, though. See what he has to say firsthand. Write it up for Georgie and she can get it entered into the National Crime Information Center in the morning. Any reason to suspect foul play?"

"Nothing specific, other than she just says he's never done this before and wouldn't just not come home or call her."

"Is his vehicle missing, too? You need to get that info out to patrol."

"Yeah, he left for work in his truck. I've got that information out. I'll give Barney a call."

"Anything else happen at the construction site after Friday night?" Conrad was itching to go down there and look around for himself, but he couldn't do that from Kentucky.

"No. Patrol kept an eye on it and never saw any breach after that."

"Did you go up there Friday night? I mean, upstairs. Did you look around? See anything?" Conrad only knew that Wink went to the site and got Cora home safely.

"I didn't go upstairs, but Tabor and Asher were up there. They said they didn't see anything." Conrad would have looked for himself.

"You'll need to stop by Monday morning and let the manager there know about the report. Have them check on things."

"Yeah, I plan to," Wink said.

"You might want to talk to some of the guys about Hollingsworth while you're there. I'm sure the mayor is going to go down there. If she doesn't think the job is getting done, she'll be doing it herself."

"Understood, Chief. He could have just decided to cut out. Maybe it's nothing."

"That may be the usual case, but you have to work it like it's real."

CHAPTER 9

"You sure are popular today," Violet Hoenigberg said to Cora with a smile as she walked up to her on the sidewalk in front of the church. "Is it my turn to talk to you now? You have a longer line than the pastor!"

Cora laughed and hugged her mentor. Violet Hoenigberg had been an elementary teacher at Peppermint Elementary for many years before Cora started working there, and she had been in the classroom next to Cora's. Although they had both retired now, they remained close friends. "Everyone wants to give me their ideas about naming the new community center. I can't possibly remember all the suggestions. Amanda will have to keep track of all that for me."

"The old popcorn factory?"

"Yes. I'm hoping to find a name the town will embrace and quit calling it the old popcorn factory."

Violet laughed and patted Cora's hand. "Oh, honey. You're fighting another uphill battle."

"Probably, but I like a challenge." Cora chuckled. Violet always spoke her mind. "How are you doing? It's good to see you out."

"I'm feeling pretty good these days, but I'm already dreading winter. My bones don't like the cold," Violet said, shuddering as the cool morning breeze ruffled her silver hair. "I thought maybe the line was forming because folks had an idea about your missing guy."

"Missing guy?" Cora said jerking her head back. "What missing guy?"

"Owen Hollingsworth," Violet said with arched eyebrows. "You didn't know?"

"No! Who told you he was missing? I just saw him Friday. He's working on the community center."

"I know. His wife, Bonita, said he didn't come home Friday night and she reported him missing. Conrad didn't tell you?"

"Conrad's out of town," Cora said frowning. "How did you hear this? Do you know Bonita?"

"No, but I saw Geraldine in the store yesterday and her granddaughter takes dance lessons from Tonya Grace. When her daughter picked up her granddaughter from class yesterday, one of the mothers of another girl in the class told her daughter that Owen was missing. She said his wife, Bonita, reported it to the police, so I thought you'd know."

"Hmm," Cora huffed. "I didn't, but maybe he turned up."

"No," Violet said shaking her head. "Nicole was sitting behind me today and she said her sister, Melody, is dating Josh Finley and he told her that Owen hasn't shown up."

"Oh, my. I hope nothing has happened to him. I don't know him well. I just met him at the construction site."

"I had him in class," Violet said with a dismissive wave of her hand. "It was before you started. He was a bit of a prankster as a young boy, not as sharp as his sister, but a good kid. He's nothing like Ruth."

"I try to visit the construction site every day they're working. I'll check in tomorrow and see if he's returned."

§

"Hi, Connie," Cora said. "I'm glad you called."

"Uh oh," Conrad said, hesitating at Cora's tone. He wanted to start walking backwards the way Briscoe did when they entered the veterinarian's office. "What's wrong?"

"Did you know we have a missing citizen?"

"Uh, well, I know, uh, I did talk to Wink. He's looking into it. He doesn't know yet if, well, exactly what the circumstances are."

"Wink hasn't called me."

"I think he's not sure, you know. Maybe he's going to show up."

"Well, the whole town knows, with the exception of me, of course."

"I'm sorry, Cora. I'm not there. I didn't know everybody knew about it or I would have called you. The wife must have told people when she was looking around for him. I would have called you if I'd known it was anything real."

"You always say that they get worked like they're real, regardless," Cora said with a sharp edge to her voice.

"You're right. I do, and it will be. Wink is doing some preliminary investigation now and I'll keep you updated. There's no need for you to worry."

"How's Kentucky?" Cora asked after an awkward silence.

"Briscoe is having a good time. He's made a friend at the training facility, a young pup that's in training here. He's out playing with him now. Did you just get home from church?"

"Yes. That's where I heard about Owen. The place was all abuzz with naming the community center. Did I tell you I put that in the paper?"

"No. What did you name it?"

"I didn't. I told the community to make suggestions, and although they're supposed to send them into Amanda, they were all giving them to me at church today."

"You asked for it," Conrad laughed. "What's wrong with just calling it the community center?"

"Not a thing. I just like a little fun," Cora smiled. "Some of the suggestions are pretty creative. I kind of like the one that Cece Fields gave me. The Spice Jar. What do you think?"

"Well, you know me. I call things what they are, and that building isn't a jar."

Cora Mae laughed. "You're always so literal. It's symbolism, Connie. Instead of being named a particular spice, which most people suggest, it's a collection of all the spices. It's a symbol of diversity in our community."

"If you say so," Conrad huffed. "Most people are going to call it the old popcorn factory, and that's probably going to drive you crazy."

"You know me so well. Have you made up with Wink?"

"Made up? I've talked to him this morning. He's okay."

"I know you felt bad that you ruined his date."

"He was wrong, and he knows it." Conrad sighed. "He underestimated my job, and now he doesn't."

"Well, I'm sure you'll be home soon since Briscoe did so well at his test yesterday. What does he have to do tomorrow?"

"Simulated seek exercises in the morning. They have a building on the facility that someone hides in and he has to enter the building and find them."

"Can he do that?"

"I feel certain he could do it if I went with him. I don't know how he'll do alone."

"He could get hurt in there by himself. I mean, in a real situation."

"Yes, but it makes it safer for officers. That's the goal for these trained police dogs. You send them in where it's dangerous for officers to go. They can move a lot faster than we can, too."

"I don't want officers or dogs to get hurt, but they could have used him Friday night at the construction site. Briscoe could have gone upstairs and caught whoever was up there. By the time Eugene got there, they were gone."

"Tabor may have interrupted them, though. If they heard cars pull up, they may not have had time to steal anything. It could be kids just sneaking around, too. The site needs to be better secured."

"I'll go down there in the morning. I need to see if they know anything about Owen and see if they have anything missing. It seems sometimes they don't know about the missing tools until they need to use them. Wink said everyone has to check out tools and put them back up. So, how is there anything around to steal? Are they not checking them back in? Or is it—"

"An inside job?" Conrad said. "That's why the construction company should be looking into security. There's a chance it's one of their own guys."

"I'll let you know what I find out. You enjoy your vacation. Briscoe is doing all the work, isn't he?"

"Yeah, but he doesn't see it as work. He gets to climb tomorrow afternoon. They have a sloping wall here, like a rocky incline. He gets to see if he can scale it. I know I can't."

"Oh, I know," Cora said laughing. "I'm doing well to get up my own porch steps!"

CHAPTER 10

"Hey, Alan," Erika Johnson said as Alan Avery opened the office trailer door to walk out with his clipboard in his hand. "The welder is scheduled today. Are we ready for her?"

"I don't think so. I don't think the build out is done. Owen screwed up that wall unit and put us behind."

"I'm going up to check with Barney. Owen isn't here yet, as far as I know, but I just saw Cheryl Pittman's truck pulling up." Erika pointed to the parking lot. "Can she start work on the other side, maybe? We need to get the beams up."

"Let me go around and check," Alan said as he walked around to the street side of the building and Erika headed up the stairs. "Hey, Finley."

"Morning," Joshua Finley said.

"Is the back support done enough for the welder to get in there today? Did you and Cy finish Friday?"

"Yeah," Finley said. "Cy is back there already. Hey, did you hear Owen is M-I-A?"

"What?"

"Yeah, Owen disappeared. Barney said nobody knows where he went."

"Disappeared when?"

"Nobody could find him all weekend. They got the police looking for him now."

"The police!"

"Yeah." Finley nodded with conviction. "His wife filed a missing person report and everything. Seems he disappeared sometime after work Friday."

"Wow," Alan said, teetering between concern and euphoria. "I didn't know anything about it."

"Where do you want us today, boss?"

"Better go check with Barney and see if he needs help. I don't think they finished Friday, and Cheryl is here. I'll have her start on this side and if you guys can get it done over there, she'll move there next."

"Okay," Finley said and then yelled for Cyrus through cupped hands as Alan turned to find Erika.

§

"But Joe, did you expect Owen to show up at the poker game?" Cora peered over Joe Barney's shoulder as he was crouched down.

"I can't say, ma'am. I wouldn't have been surprised either way. I knew he'd be late if he did show, but he liked hanging around that derby. So, if he could work on cars, he would have stayed after instead of showing up at Sammy's house. I wasn't worried or nothin'."

"When did Owen's wife call you?"

"Saturday morning. She told me he didn't come home Friday. Even then though, I just thought maybe he worked on cars real late. I told her maybe he was at the garage and didn't want to come in real late and wake her."

"Did they have marital problems?" Cora whispered and looked around. She hated to ask, but there was no delicate way to say it.

"Doesn't everybody?" Joe Barney chuckled and stood up to reach for his laser. "No offense, ma'am, but he didn't talk about that much. Bonita was always real sweet to me when I was around. She's a nice lady."

"I'm sure she is," Cora said with a furrowed brow. "I certainly didn't mean to imply otherwise. I just thought maybe they'd had a little spat or something. Perhaps he's just giving her some space and she's worried. Do you think something bad has happened to him? I mean, you know him better than anyone here. Would he do something like this? Just go off without telling anyone?"

"I don't know," Joe said shaking his head. "You never know what's going on with people, do you?"

"Something's off," Joshua Finley said walking over to grab the broom. "I haven't known him as long as Barney has, but he's been acting funny lately. Screwin' up at work, fightin' with Avery, actin' weird."

"Have you seen this too, Joe?" Cora raised both eyebrows and stared at Joe Barney.

"He's been acting okay to me. I mean, he's been getting into it with Avery. They just don't get along," Joe said as he moved further away to crouch down again.

"Owen was my union mentor when I first started," Joshua said. "He taught me how to frame. Taught a lot of these other guys, too. Now he's making lazy mistakes? Doesn't make sense to me."

"Hmm," Cora said, stepping back to speak to Cyrus McDaniel, but found he had just walked away.

"Would Owen go to the derby alone? The rest of you, you don't like the derby?"

"Alvarez and Knapp went to the derby before they came to Sammy's. They didn't see Owen there, but it's a big place." Joshua shrugged his shoulders and pulled a pencil from behind his ear to mark the stud where his measuring tape was stretched.

"You were late getting to Sammy's," Barney said with a snide glance.

"I was," Josh said with a curt nod to Cora. "I had a date."

Joe Barney glanced over his shoulder and grinned mischievously at Joshua.

"Do you remember what those are, old man?" Josh said, leaning down and directing his joke at Barney while they both laughed.

Cora ignored their banter. "So, Owen would just go alone to the derby and sit there, and watch cars smash into each other?" She really didn't understand the dynamics of a demolition derby, but she thought the concept was battered cars ram into each other until they could no longer run.

"He didn't sit in the stands usually," Joe Barney said. "He worked in some of the pit crews, so he was down on the field, on the side."

"Ah, I see. Well, I don't want to delay you any further. I hope we hear from Owen soon and that nothing bad has happened. Have a good day, gentlemen." Cora wiggled her fingers in goodbye as they all returned to work. She needed to find out more about this derby work and headed down the stairs in deep thought.

§

"Good morning, Miss Johnson," Wink said with a bow of his head. "Could I speak with you for a moment?" Wink had asked the workers on the site to direct him to the manager and he had been guided to the trailer door.

"Certainly, Officer. Come in," Erika said, removing her hard hat from the visitor's chair. "Have a seat. Are you here about Owen Hollingsworth?"

"Ah, well, that," Wink stammered. "I guess you've heard. He didn't show today, did he?"

"No, but the guys told me that his wife called them this weekend. Nobody seems to know where he is. I haven't seen him since Friday, either."

"Well, the other issue... We received a call Friday evening that someone was in the building upstairs. I wanted to let you know about that and have you check for any missing items. The officers arrived and whoever was up there took off. We just want to make sure that you aren't missing anything."

"Yes, the mayor told me. We haven't discovered anything missing yet," Erika said. "I'll be sure and file a report with you, if I do though."

"I'm Officer Hobson, by the way," Wink said, extending his hand to shake.

"Erika Johnson. It's nice to meet you. The mayor told us that the Chief was out of town and you might stop by."

"I know the mayor likes to check in on things." Wink forced a smile. "Is there any reason that someone should be here after hours or over the weekend?"

"No. I wouldn't say it never happens because someone from the firm might want to do a walk around or something might get delivered really early, but it's not routine. We start early but everyone clears out in the afternoon. We don't work at night at all."

"You might want to secure the site a bit more. It's pretty easy to get in here at night." Wink pointed to the side of the building. "The officers said they just moved a sheet of plywood that someone had already pried loose."

"Yeah, we could do better," Erika said nodding. "We've had vandals before, but truthfully, I thought everything was pretty quiet in Spicetown and we wouldn't have any trouble at all. That's not been the case."

"You aren't from here."

"No, I live in Paxton. My jobs have all been over there, and we've had people breaking into our sites. We'll try to do better tonight about sealing things up."

"All right then," Wink said, turning to leave. "You let us know if you need anything."

"I sure will."

Wink pushed open the trailer door to go down the steps as he put his cap back on.

"Good morning, Wink," Cora said as she walked up with her pink hard hat on her head. "How are you today? The weather has cleared up, thank goodness."

"Morning, Mayor," Wink said, smiling at her hard hat as she took it off. "Is everything going well on the site today?"

"Appears to be," Cora said. "Are you heading back?"

"Yeah, I just talked to Miss Johnson."

"Well, if you've got a minute…"

"Sure," Wink said uneasily.

"Let me drop off my hat and we'll get some coffee."

"Sure, Mayor. I could use a cup."

Cora hopped up the steps to the trailer and said her goodbyes to Erika as she hung her hard hat on the hook inside the door. "I'll see you later, Erika. Have a good day."

"You too," Erika hollered as Cora shut the door.

"I've been talking to some of the guys this morning," Cora said as she started to stroll downtown and glanced back for Wink to join her. "I didn't know if you had talked to anyone about Owen yet, but I thought maybe we should compare notes."

"Maybe I need to make notes," Wink said with a chuckle. "I've talked to his wife and Joe Barney, but that's all."

"Well, I think I have a handle on where everyone here was on Friday night. I don't know if that will help, but it gives us a starting point."

"I definitely need to take notes," Wink said frowning.

"So glad to see a man admit he needs to write something down once in a while," Cora said with a smile. "You know your boss; he thinks he can remember everything I say and refuses to make notes. I keep telling him his life will be easier if he makes a list."

"You don't need to convince me, Mayor. And I know the Chief makes notes. He just keeps them a secret from you."

Cora tossed her head back and laughed. "I knew it!"

CHAPTER 11

"So, what have you heard?" Sandy Teague said to Mitzi Boyle as she combed through her hair. "I know Owen Hollingsworth is missing. Josh called me last night and told me. Has Wink said anything?"

"I thought you and Joshua Finley broke up. Didn't you tell me that just last week when you came in to make this appointment?" Mitzi laughed at Sandy's guilty expression she saw in the beauty shop wall mirror.

"Hey, that was last week. We got back together Friday night. He took me out to dinner and.... You know. He's really sweet when he's in trouble."

"Well," Mitzi said, "it don't mean he won't get in trouble again, but I'm glad he's sweet to you."

"Thank you," Sandy said with a chuckle. "So, did Wink say anything? Anybody know where Owen went?"

"I haven't talked to Wink today," Mitzi said.

"Well, I asked Loudene earlier," Louise said as she spun her empty chair around when Teresa Barney walked up holding a damp towel on her head. "Have a seat."

"What did she say?" Mitzi said, pausing with a brush in her hand.

"She said she didn't see Owen Friday night. She thought he would come work in their pit crew at the derby, but he didn't show up. They just thought he was busy or was working in somebody else's crew, though. She wasn't worried, but she had been seeing him pretty regularly. He comes by her husband's garage sometimes on Saturday, too. He loves to tinker with those old cars."

"Josh said they thought he might come to poker Friday night after the derby, but he didn't show."

"My ex-husband runs around with Owen Hollingsworth all the time," Teresa said as Louise tucked a dry towel around her neck.

"I didn't know you still talked to Joe. Are you guys on better terms now?" Louise combed through Teresa's damp hair and sectioned it off for a trim.

"Child support," Teresa said grinning. "He still owes me, but he's working on catching up."

"Ah," Mitzi said as she ran her fingers through Sandy's locks. "You want the back to stay long?"

"Yes, just a trim, please," Sandy said. "How old is your boy now, Teresa?"

"He'll be eighteen in November, but Joe is way behind. Last winter was rough on him. He didn't get a lot of work. He had car trouble last night and I picked him up. That's how I got my child support."

"Josh said Owen was having problems at work, so maybe he just had enough of it." Sandy shrugged her shoulders as Mitzi guided her over to the shampoo bowls.

"I just can't see that," Louise said, looking at Teresa through the mirror. "Owen's wife, Bonita, comes in here and she's as sweet as they come. She talks about Owen and they seem really happy together. I can't believe Owen would just up and leave her. I don't know him personally, but—"

"No, I agree," Teresa said. "Joe's known them both for a long time and he's never talked like they fight or anything."

"Did Joe seem worried?" Louise pulled the wet hair between her fingers to cut.

"He was kind of anxious, but he didn't mention anything."

"Well, I hope they find him soon," Mitzi said as she turned off the water spray and began massaging in shampoo. "And I hope he's all right."

§

"What do you mean you have a map?"

"It's all here, Chief," Wink said. "It's like a wall mural. It's not that big, but it shows all the parties and exactly where they were with little dotted lines to show the times they moved around in colored ink. It's incredible."

"Cora's been busy."

"Yeah, she's talked to everybody, and I didn't even tell you about the index cards!"

"Oh?" Conrad closed his eyes and sighed.

"That's where all the little facts are that she used to put this map together."

"Good grief."

"No, it's not like that," Wink said in Cora's defense. "It's incredible. Best thing I've ever seen. I don't know why I never thought of it. This case has a lot of people involved. It's the only way to keep track of all of them. She's a genius."

Conrad laughed and vowed never to let Cora know of that new title. "She's very detail-oriented."

"Sure is," Wink said. "And it's a godsend with this group. There's like a dozen guys, all going different places at different times, and they all saw Owen Hollingsworth at a different time or place. It would take me a week to do this."

"Now you know the secret to running Spicetown," Conrad said with a chuckle. "It's all in the notes."

CHAPTER 12

"I smell Amanda Morgan's famous chili," Louise called out in a sing-song voice from the door as she hung up her coat. "This is wonderful, honey. What made you decide to cook tonight?"

"I was hungry, and I know you get home late on Mondays. It just sounded good."

"Well, it smells delicious. Hymie?" Louise yelled out into the living room. "I'm going to make myself a salad. Do you want one?"

"No thanks."

"How was City Hall today? The shop was busy all day long, and my feet hurt." Louise pulled open the refrigerator to gather her salad supplies.

"Pretty normal day for me," Amanda said as she placed bowls on the counter.

"Everybody was talking about Owen Hollingsworth disappearing. Mitzi said Wink still doesn't know anything."

Amanda recognized right away that Louise was fishing for information. "I haven't heard any updates."

"Wink is a great guy, but I don't know if he knows what to do when something this serious happens. Is the Chief coming back soon?"

"I really don't know when he'll be back," Amanda said.

"I'm sure Cora is on top of this. Maybe the Chief can help by phone. Can they check his credit cards and stuff like that?"

"I'm not sure," Amanda said as she ladled chili into a bowl.

"In a town this small, maybe we can't do all that fancy stuff you see on TV. The guys at the construction site don't know anything, either." Louise reached up for drinking glasses and opened the drawer for silverware.

"You had guys from the construction site in the beauty shop today?" Hymie stretched his tall frame out with his hands behind his head and groaned as he walked into the kitchen.

"No, silly," Louise said with a teasing wave. "I had wives, girlfriends, and even ex-wives in the shop. Their guys don't know anything. He just evaporated. It's so weird. He may turn up twenty years from now in Bryan's garden!"

Amanda's body went rigid from shock and Louise cackled at her own joke.

"Not funny, Lou," Hymie said with a concerned frown. "Let's just hope he returns home safe and sound. Maybe it's all just a misunderstanding."

"I hope so," Amanda said quietly as she placed the bowls and spoons on the table.

"My new vet tech, Lily, said she knows Owen and his wife. They live next door to her mom." Hymie reached for the crackers. "She said when she was in vet tech school and lived at home, Owen's wife asked her a million questions about her little dog. She's not a current patient of ours, though."

"His wife has been in the shop. She's very sweet, but on the quiet side. I don't know Owen. Do you, honey?"

"No," Amanda said.

"I bet Cora knows him. She knows everybody. Teresa Barney told me that her ex-husband Joe is pretty worried. He's close friends with Owen." Louise poked an ice cube down in her tea glass. "Apparently, Owen was expected at a poker game Friday night and he didn't show. Sandy said Josh told her Joe Barney got to the game late and was surprised that Owen had never shown up."

"I saw Joe Barney Friday," Hymie said as he cocked his head. "He was driving out of town on North Road, just past Bryan's house, as I was coming back from the Beck's farm. It was almost dark, but he saw me and waved. He has a couple of dogs that I see."

"Did the calf at the Beck's place do okay?" Amanda asked. Her dad had helped with the birth over the weekend but told them that it was touch and go.

"She perked right up Sunday, they said. I talked to Beck this morning. It looks like she'll be okay." Hymie's broad smile was contagious. Amanda enjoyed his stories from the office so much more than her mother's shop gossip.

§

Mitzi glared at Wink as she reached for the bag he was carrying. "Are you going to run off before I get done eating?"

"I can't promise," Wink said. "You know I didn't do it intentionally, but I never know what's going to happen. Until the Chief comes back, I have to be available. Bringing dinner to you seemed the best way to deal with the situation. Then if I get called out, you'll be safe at home with a good meal."

Mitzi shifted her weight to one leg and propped her hand at her waist. "It's not exactly the best offer I've ever had, but I guess you owe me a meal."

"When the Chief comes back, things will be different."

"Yeah, you'll be back working nights," Mitzi huffed as she opened the containers of food Wink had brought in and arranged them on the table.

"Not every night. My nights off are all yours."

Mitzi blushed before leaning over the food cartons to give Wink a kiss. "I hope so."

"That I can promise."

"So, how was your day?" Mitzi pulled plates from the cupboard and set the table. "The shop was busy."

"I went down to the construction site this morning. I had to check on security down there," Wink said, spreading a napkin across his lap.

"Did you interview everybody about Owen Hollingsworth? Has anybody seen him?"

"No, I don't know where he is," Wink said. "Do you have ketchup?"

"You don't sound very concerned. Do you think the guy just left town on his own?" Mitzi sat the ketchup down in front of Wink and pulled out her chair.

"I don't see any evidence of foul play, really. Maybe he did just leave."

"The girls at the shop disagree. They know Owen's wife and some of the guys at the site. No one thinks Owen took off."

"We don't have any leads. We're just trying to track his last movements. That's all we can do right now." Wink squeezed the ketchup on his plate.

"Teresa Barney was in the shop today and she said her ex-husband is Owen's best friend and he doesn't know where he is."

Wink nodded and chewed.

"His best friend and his wife know nothing. Doesn't that indicate possible foul play?"

"Nope," Wink said. "It indicates he's secretive. Foul play would be like—" Wink jumped when his cell phone rang. "Just a second. I've got to take this."

Mitzi rolled her eyes as Wink pulled the napkin off his lap and walked into her living room to talk.

"Sorry, honey. I've got to go," Wink said, dashing back in the room to give Mitzi a peck on the cheek.

"But what about your food? Don't you want to take it with you?"

"No time for that now." Wink pulled open the front door with one arm in the sleeve of his jacket.

"But what happened?"

"They found the guy's truck," Wink said as he rushed down the steps.

"Hollingsworth?"

"Yeah," Wink said opening his door. "I'll call you tomorrow, babe."

"Was he in it?"

Wink waved as he backed his car out into the road to turn.

§

"Do you want help with the dishes, Mom?" Amanda carried dishes from the table to the kitchen counter.

"I'm just going to put them in the dishwasher."

"I think it needs to be emptied. Let me do that while you rinse everything."

Hymie Morgan was already settled in his favorite chair in the family room. "That movie you wanted to see comes on at eight."

"Okay, honey—" Louise searched for her cell phone when she heard her xylophone ring tone.

"Hello... Oh hi, Mitzi. Is everything okay? ... Oh, really.... Interesting.... Thanks, hon. See you tomorrow."

Louise put her phone by her purse and picked up the last of the dishes on the table.

"That was Mitzi," Louise said, and Amanda nodded.

"Is everything okay?"

"Yeah, she was trying to have dinner with Wink again," Louise paused to chuckle. "And he got another call."

"That's just because the Chief is gone. It will get better."

"I know, but this is interesting, at least. Wink got a call because they found that guy's truck, Hollingsworth."

"Really? Where was it?"

"She didn't say, but she said he must not have been in it. She said Wink just said the truck was found."

"Still," Amanda said. "That will maybe give them some clues. Hopefully, it will help."

"Maybe Wink will call her back tonight and we'll find out."

Amanda leaned over the dishwasher and removed the plates from the rack as her mother turned on the garbage disposal.

"I wonder if the truck was in the lake," Louise said when she turned off the water.

"Why would you think that?" Amanda slid the stacked plates into the cabinet.

"Mitzi said Wink turned north when he left her house. Mitzi lives on Red Pepper Road and there are only two streets to choose if you turn north away from her house. Wink would have been going out where Bryan lives or out Eagle Bay Road to the lake. He would have turned the other way if he were going back to town."

"I'm sure we'll find out soon enough," Amanda said as she began to load the emptied dishwasher with the bowls her mother had rinsed. "The paper tomorrow will have all that information."

"The paper? Oh, honey, I don't wait on The Spicetown Star. Word of mouth is the only way you find out anything around this town."

"It's starting," Hymie yelled from his recliner.

"I'm coming," Louise yelled back. "Do you mind finishing this for me, honey? I don't want to miss the start of the movie."

"Sure, Mom."

CHAPTER 13

"Good morning, Amanda," Cora Mae said as she struggled to remove her coat. "Have you heard the latest?"

"Good morning, Mayor," Amanda said. "Do you mean about the missing man's truck?"

"I do," Cora said as she walked through Amanda's office to her own. "Did your mom tell you?"

"Yeah, well someone called her and I was there, so she told me." Amanda stood in Cora's office doorway.

"I expected that. I heard from a concerned citizen who called me at home last night, and she is a patron of your mother's."

"The police didn't call you?"

Cora dropped her purse in the bottom drawer of her desk and made a growling sound. "Not yet."

"Oh," Amanda said sensing Cora's frustration. "Well, maybe they thought it was too late. Do you know where it was? I just heard it was north of town."

"I can't say for sure, but the caller said it was a few miles out on North Road, just past Bryan's house. When you go over the hill at Mavis Bell's house, there's a dirt road to the right. The truck was parked down there."

"That's an odd place. Is there a house on that dirt road?"

"No. It's just a farm entrance. I think they drive the trucks to the field on that road, but it doesn't go to anyone's house. All that land is leased for crops."

"Are you going down to the construction site this morning?" Amanda turned back toward her desk as she heard her phone ring.

"After I check my email," Cora said as Amanda scurried off when the phone rang on her desk.

Amanda glanced at her vibrating cell phone on the corner of her desk. "Good morning."

"Hi, honey. Sorry to bother you, but I'm going to have to cancel dinner tonight," Bryan said. "I've got to drive up to Hillsboro and pick up some trees. My order was messed up and they were delivered up there."

"Shouldn't whoever delivered them bring them to you?"

"Yeah, but then I've got to wait all week on them, and they'll probably die. I've been looking for them since Friday and just found out where they are."

"Do you have someone to keep an eye on things?" Bryan ran the Stotlar Nursery from his home and usually took care of things during the week by himself. Amanda helped him on Saturdays.

"I called Mavis and she's going to come by after lunch. She's working at Chervil Drugs this morning, but said she was free in the afternoon. I won't be back until almost dark, though."

"Okay, we can have dinner another night. Have you seen police out by your place?" Amanda cupped her hand around the receiver and lowered her voice. "Did you know that guy's truck was found just down the road from you?"

"Was it a blue truck? I saw one go by on a tow truck this morning."

"I don't know what color it was, but they found it last night. You didn't see anything going on last night?"

"No police cars that I noticed. Nothing out of the ordinary."

"They found it late, after dark," Amanda said. "You would have been closed. The guy wasn't in the truck, though."

"So, he has just disappeared into thin air?"

"Seems so. Did you see anybody walking? Maybe he broke down out there."

"I did see a guy walking, but it was getting dark and I was inside."

"That might have been him!" Amanda jumped as Officer Harold Hobson walked behind her and pointed his finger at the mayor's office door. Amanda smiled and nodded.

"You should probably tell the police what you saw. You may have been the last person to see him."

"I hope not. I didn't even really look. It was just a guy, and I don't know what I'd tell them. I didn't think it was anything."

"Well, think about it. See if you remember anything. Officer Hobson is in with the mayor now, so I've got to go, but I'll tell the mayor. I'm sure she'll say that you need to think hard and write down what you remember about what he was wearing, what time it was, and stuff like that."

"Geez," Bryan said with a breathy sigh. "I'll try."

§

"Morning, Mayor," Wink said, tipping his hat in Cora's doorway. "Miss Morgan is on the phone. Do you have a minute?"

"You are early today, Officer Hobson." Cora peered at Wink over her reading glasses.

"I wanted to catch you before you went to the construction site today."

"Well, you caught me," Cora said sitting back and removing her glasses. "I was just getting ready to go down there."

"I came by to let you know—"

"That you found Owen's truck?" Cora folded her hands on her desk.

"Yes, ma'am," Wink said clutching his hat in his hand. "How did you hear? It was found abandoned out on North Road but—"

"Owen wasn't in it," Cora said nodding. "Yes, I know."

"Sorry, Mayor. I didn't want to call you so late last night, but I wanted you to hear it from me. Did the Chief call you already?"

"No, I haven't talked to the Chief." Cora shook her head sadly and looked down at her hands. "Think about it Wink. Who else have you told?"

"It just happened last night."

"And where were you last night?" Cora said and then immediately held her hands up with her palms out. "I'm not asking, and I don't mean to get into your personal life, Wink, but you've got to be more careful with this kind of information."

"Ma'am? I'm not sure—"

"You told your date last night, Wink," Cora said leaning forward and watched as the realization registered across Wink's face. "And she told somebody, who told somebody, and I'm sure it was all over town before the sun came up. Yeah, I heard all about it, but not the way I should have."

"Oh, gosh. Mayor, I'm sorry. I didn't even think. I was running to jump in my car and you're right. I did tell her why, and I know better. I didn't even think about her sharing the information. I'm sorry, and I promise it won't happen again."

"I'm not the one you'll probably have to convince," Cora said. She wasn't going to be the one to tell Conrad. "Do you want to walk with me? I'm headed down to the construction site now. We can talk on the way."

CHAPTER 14

Cy McDaniels leaned over a stack of lumber to pick through the pile for just the right piece of trim he needed. Jumping at the sound of a ringing phone, he stood upright and looked around, but didn't see any other workers nearby. Cupping both of his hands around his mouth, he yelled as loud as he could. "Anybody lose a phone?"

Laughing, he picked up the wood he was carrying and walked to the front of the Community Center where Cora and Wink were standing. "Morning, Mayor."

Cora looked over her shoulder and smiled. "Good morning, Cy. How are you today?"

"Oh, just fine." Cy chuckled, tossing his thumb over his shoulder to point to the side of the building. "Somebody's lost their phone though."

Cora frowned.

"I just heard a phone ringing in the dumpster over there. It must be another prank."

Cora nodded and smiled. "You have a good day, Cy."

"Sure will, ma'am." Cy tipped his head in a bow and headed over to the stairway with his trim over his shoulder.

"The guys are always playing jokes on each other," Cora shook her head in mock disapproval. "My hat's in the trailer. You'll need one, too." Cora edged Wink towards the trailer door. Wink groaned and slipped his ball cap off, folding it to stuff in his back pocket. Cora knocked on the trailer door, but no one answered.

"They must be out already. I'll just grab some hard hats."

Wink looked around at the open front of the building. "So, what's going on out here exactly?"

"Oh, it's going to be beautiful," Cora said, handing a yellow hard hat to Wink. "They're building the front out with iron beams, and there'll be a glass roof canopy that goes to the parking lot so people can get out of the weather. It's a very modern looking design. That's the only major change to the outside. All the other work is on the interior. They've cleaned out the center of the building completely now and there'll be a large open space with a stage at one end for events, but the front of the building has some office spaces for ticket sales. The restrooms have all been expanded. It really wasn't changed that much. Most of the center of the building was a large open floor already, and we expect to be able to use it by October."

"So, what exactly did Owen Hollingsworth do here?" Wink asked.

"Well, he's a general carpenter. He was framing out the office space in the front to extend the area where the canopy will connect to make it strong enough to carry the glass ceiling. I think he did some work on the restroom walls because we expanded those, too. He usually worked with Joe Barney, but there are others here that are general carpenters as well. Every time I visited, he seemed to be with Joe. I think they're pretty close friends."

"Yes, that's what his wife said. She said he's worked with Joe for years."

"Let's go upstairs and see what's going on today. I'm sure either Alan or Erika are up there." Cora led Wink up the steps in the front of the building and they walked toward the noise of hammers and saws. Voices could be heard in every corner.

"Good morning everyone. How is everyone today?" Cora called out.

Several of the guys turned around nodded their head, shared their greetings, and Alan waved as Wink walked up.

"Mr. Avery," Wink said. "If you have a minute this morning, I'd like to chat with you." Although Cora's map and index cards had been very detailed on the whereabouts of each of the workers, Wink hadn't had a chance to talk to Alan Avery on Monday.

"Sure thing, Officer Hobson. I'm happy to help."

Cora glanced at Wink. "I'm going to look around. I'll pick you up at the trailer."

§

Wink nodded and followed Alan Avery down the steps. Once they were settled in the trailer office, Wink took a chair next to Alan's desk and pulled out a notepad. "I've got a few questions I'd like to ask about Owen Hollingsworth."

"Do you have any leads? We still haven't heard anything. He hasn't called in. I called the union yesterday and asked them if they'd heard from him, but they haven't."

"Oh, he's a union guy?"

"All the workers are union members, but Owen was pretty tight with the union. He's an on-site rep. He's worked with them for years, and he does a lot of training for them. I think he stayed in pretty close touch with the union most of the time."

"If you have a name and number, I'll give them a call as well."

"Sure, I do." Alan pulled out a notepad from his desk and wrote down a name and phone number to hand to Wink.

"One of the things I wanted to ask you about is Owen's work. I've been told that he had some problems at work. He was making some mistakes?"

"He was," Alan said. "He was showing up late for work and his work was not up to par. I haven't worked with Owen before, but everybody tells me that he was a great worker."

"But you didn't find that to be true?"

"His work was substandard, and his behavior was disappointing. We did have words about it several times."

"But you didn't fire him?"

"Well, no. It doesn't work that way. The union contract specifies how we can deal with performance and conduct issues. I had some of both with Owen, and we had a lot of discussions. I couldn't really do much more than that."

Wink frowned.

"He delayed our project more than once because we had to take out some of the work he did. That's what they're working on up there right now. We had to take out a wall that he did last week, and the guys are replacing it. I don't know why his work ethic has changed, but I've had a lot of problems with Owen Hollingsworth."

"So, what does the union say?"

"Oh, they just defend him. It's all about me. I am a terrible person because I expect good work from the employees. It's always my fault, somehow. That's just the usual way they are. They are trying to protect his job at any cost. They don't care about the integrity of the project."

"You sound like you resent that."

"I don't think resent is the right word. It is frustrating to me because the work that we do is important and if you do it poorly, you can endanger somebody's life."

"You mean the building will fall in?"

Alan laughed. "Not specifically, but when you don't take care of tools and someone else picks them up, that person is at risk. When you don't do your work right, the people that have to come behind you and do their part have problems. We are on a time schedule. Redoing all of his work was setting us back. Some workers have specific duties that you have to schedule. When we schedule someone to come in and they can't do their job yet because he's made us late, we have to pay that worker to be idle. It all adds up to lost time, lost money, and high risk."

"Sounds like Owen shouldn't have been on this job, but you couldn't fire him," Wink said.

"No, I couldn't. The construction company didn't support that, and the union fought it. For some reason, it seemed to me that they both protected

Owen. I don't know why. I don't know why they would want to take that risk."

"I also heard that you didn't like Owen," Wink said, lifting the eyebrow over his good eye.

"Oh, it's not personal, not at all. He seemed like a nice guy. Most of the other guys liked him. He was easygoing and seemed to get along with everyone. It wasn't personal. People don't understand that when you're in management, you have to demand quality work and call people out when they aren't doing quality work. I'm doing my job. They all think it means I don't like him, but that's just not the case. I've had some great workers that I didn't like, and I've had some poor workers that I did. One has nothing to do with the other.

"I get that," Wink said. "So, was Owen in trouble on Friday?"

"Well, we did talk at the end of the day. I had him come to my office before he clocked out. It wasn't a formal discussion. The union wasn't here, but we did talk about him showing up late for work. I also cautioned him once again about putting up his tools. He checks out tools and doesn't put them up, then they turn up stolen. When I call him on it, he always tells me he didn't check out those tools."

"Maybe he didn't," Wink said. "Could somebody else be doing it and using his name?"

"Sure. They could be, but his coworkers tell me he checked them out or that he was seen using them, so I'm not inclined to believe him. All the missing tools were in Owen's name, all but one. I don't think he stole them. I think he just left them out. People sneaking in here at night find the stuff and take it. It only costs the union money. The union buys most of those tools. They are specialty items that we've had stolen."

"Was he using the tool that Donny McBride got hurt with?" Wink asked.

"Donny was hurt by a saw that everyone uses. I can't specifically link Owen to any of the injuries. There's no way to know who had the tool right before the injury happened."

"But what about the floorboards? I remember in the beginning you had an unusual situation where there was a weakness in the second floor that hadn't been there the day before. You had a worker injured then, didn't you?"

"Yes. That was a freak accident. We still don't know how that happened. We don't have any explanation." Alan shrugged his shoulders and sat back in his chair.

"So, what was Owen's state of mind when he left Friday? Was he upset?"

"No. He seemed to know that I couldn't do anything to him. He was very relaxed when we talked. In the beginning, when things started going wrong, he got heated, but after the union meeting, I guess he knew that I didn't have any support to discipline or fire him. He just shrugged his shoulders and didn't seem to care that I was upset. In fact, I heard the guys joke about it on the floor. They said Owen was going to get me fired for harassment."

"Does Erika feel the same way?"

"As project manager, she doesn't get involved in the day-to-day supervision, but she's aware of the problems that I've had with Owen.

"Do you know Owen's wife, Bonita?"

"Not personally, she's never been down here. I didn't know Owen before this job. I think some of the guys know his wife. She called us yesterday and Erika talked to her."

"What kind of vehicle does he drive to work?"

"An old blue truck. A few times he came with Barney, Joe Barney. I guess his truck was getting worked on and Joe gave him a ride. Those days he was actually on time," Alan said with wide eyes.

"Do you know what made him chronically late to work?"

"He never gave me any explanation, really. Sometimes he'd say his wife needed him or his wife wasn't well."

"Do you see any way that his disappearance could be linked to the job?" Wink got to root of his concerns.

"No. I don't. He seemed happy-go-lucky."

"Did he have any problems with any of the other workers here? Do you know of anyone who didn't like Owen?"

"Max Alvarez had a problem with him in the beginning. I know they argued, but I don't know the specifics. Later, I saw they were friends, so they must have mended those fences. Owen wasn't a mean guy. If he said something to offend Max, it was probably unintentional. Max can be a little intense sometimes."

"So other than Joe Barney, who was Owen close to?"

"All the guys do things as a group. I hear them talk about it and make plans. I don't think anyone's left out. They all seem to get along."

"Has there been anyone on the job site that is unusual? Maybe only comes for a day or two? Someone new? Someone they don't know well?"

"Cheryl Pittman is our welder, and she only comes in when we have a job for her. They all seem to know her, though. They all seem to be comfortable working with each other. Some jobs you get a lot of fighting.

You get workers that complain about each other and they fight all the time. It's not like that here. This job has gone really smooth, except for Owen. He's been my only problem."

"It seems very strange that he's a trainer and a seasoned worker that everyone thinks highly of, and then all of a sudden on this job he can't perform," Wink said. "What could cause that?"

"I've asked myself that question a million times. I don't know. I think the guys wonder the same thing."

"Hmm," Wink said. "Well, I appreciate your time. I'll let you get back to work now. If you think of anything, please give us a call." Wink handed Alan one of his business cards. "I take it you didn't find anything stolen? I didn't hear from you yesterday."

"No, nothing has turned up, but sometimes we don't notice right away. The second floor was a little messy Monday morning. We had all the trash swept to the center of the room and Monday I noticed that it was a mess. Someone was upstairs Friday night. Maybe it was just kids."

"Have you asked the construction company about hiring night security?"

"I think Erika talked to them."

"Did you ever say you wished Owen would never come back to work?" Wink cocked his head to the side. Cora had written that on one of her statement cards. "Did you actually say that, Mr. Avery?"

Alan hung his head in shame. "I wouldn't wish anything bad to happen to Owen. I was probably frustrated and yeah, I may have said that. There were several times when I was pulling my hair out trying to figure out what to do about him. I didn't mean it that way."

"Okay," Wink said. "I know what you mean."

CHAPTER 15

Cora came downstairs and saw Wink leaving the trailer. "Did you talk to Alan?"
"Yes."
"Did you find out anything?" Cora leaned forward to try and catch Wink's eye as he stared at the ground.
"No."
"Wink Hobson, can you be any more pedantic?"
"What? Oh, I'm sorry, Mayor. What did you ask?"
"What did Alan say?"
"Oh, sorry. I asked him about his relationship with Owen. He said they got along okay, but his work was bad. He's spent a lot of time talking to him about his poor work and being late, but he didn't hate the guy. He's just being a boss."
"Did he see Owen leave Friday?"
"He talked to Owen Friday night, but he said Owen wasn't upset when he left. It doesn't seem to have anything to do with the job. If he's disappeared, it must be a personal issue."

"Did you ask him about missing tools from Friday night?"

"They haven't found anything missing."

"It seems odd," Cora said.

"You know, Avery talked like Owen is being protected." Wink squinted into the sun as they started walking down the sidewalk towards City Hall.

"Protected?"

"He said he can't do anything about Owen's poor work habits. At first, I thought it was just because Alan's a young guy. It's hard to supervise older workers when you're a young guy, but after talking to him, I don't think that's the case. I think Alan's as confused as we are."

"So, what do you think about the wife? I haven't spoken to her yet," Cora said as they turned the corner at Fennel Street.

"She says they don't have any problems. There was no fight. She expected him home by bedtime and I asked her what bedtime meant and she said by midnight. Usually she was up that late and he knew that he wouldn't wake her if he came in before that. She expected him to go to the Demolition derby and she knew there was a Friday night poker game. When it got late, she thought he had stopped by Sammy Lowe's house to see the guys. She didn't get worried until one o'clock in the morning."

"Why didn't she call the police then?"

"She thought she couldn't report a missing person until they'd been gone for 48 hours," Wink said, flinging his arms out to his sides. "People watch too much TV."

"That's a shame," Cora said. "At least patrol could have been on the lookout for something unusual if they'd known she expected him home by then. Have you talked to the demolition derby people? Is there a ticket taker or any cameras out there?"

"No luck with that yet."

"What if we put something in the paper? We could ask if anyone saw him Friday night?"

"I'll have to ask the Chief about that. I don't know if he'd want to do something like that."

"It's difficult to plot a disappearance if you don't know where they disappeared from," Cora said. "It might help us find out if he actually made it to the derby."

"Right now, it looks like Alan Avery may be the last person that saw him."

"When I was making my notes, I noticed most of the guys went home before they went to the poker game. I would expect Owen would want to clean up and change clothes, maybe eat dinner, before he went to the demolition derby."

"I asked his wife about that. She said Owen would go straight to the derby. He got dirty out there working with the cars, so he didn't worry about it and he just got something to eat at the concessions. The derby starts at six o'clock."

"Hmm," Cora said. "I guess that makes sense, but his truck being out on North Road doesn't make any sense."

"Well, he obviously got in his truck and left the construction site Friday night."

"Or maybe not," Cora said holding her index finger up. "Maybe he didn't drive it out there."

"I guess," Wink said frowning. "You think someone stole his truck and ditched it?"

"Why would they ditch it?" Cora said, grabbing Wink's forearm. "You did say it started, right? Maybe they were hiding it."

Wink stopped and wrinkled his forehead in confusion.

"Don't mind me," Cora said, patting his arm. "I'm just thinking out loud."

"Technically...hmm."

"Keep me updated, Wink," Cora said, stopping to cross Paprika Parkway and turning to face Wink. "I don't like to hear things from the street. I know how prolific the gossip is, but that's not the way I like to get my information."

"I understand, Mayor."

"If the Chief didn't explain that to you, let me tell you up front. I do expect to know what's going on in this town. I know I'm not a police officer and I'm not a member of the police force, but they are under my purview and I do expect to know."

"Yes, ma'am."

"So, when you have updates, you find clues, you find witnesses, you find trucks, I expect to be the second person you call. I don't want to hear it on the sidewalk in front of church or in the beauty shop chair."

"I understand, Mayor, and that won't happen again. I'll let you know immediately."

"You can always text me if you're in a rush. A text is better than me not knowing what's going on in my own town."

Wink nodded his head as they crossed the street when the light changed. "You have a good day, Mayor."

Cora turned to go towards City Hall as Wink scurried back to the PD.

§

"I'm back," Cora Mae said as she struggled to get her coat off in Amanda's outer office.

"Did everything go okay?" Amanda stood up with a frown of concern.

"Yes, everything is coming along well at the community center. Why do you ask?"

"Your face is flushed. I thought maybe—"

"Oh, it's just the wind. It's chilly out there this morning and we walked into the wind." Her frustrations with Wink's poor reporting skills may have raised her blood pressure a bit, too.

Amanda relaxed and returned to her seat as Cora hung her jacket on the coat tree. "I talked to Bryan while you were out. He told me he saw a man walking down his road Friday night."

"Really?" Cora said. "When was that?"

"He said it was dark and then he said it was just getting dark. He doesn't know who it was. I told him to write up everything he could remember and to try to figure out what time it was, so we can report it. It may be nothing and he didn't really pay attention because he said it wasn't all that unusual."

"You did exactly right, dear. You never know, it might be the clue that solves the whole case."

"I didn't tell him that," Amanda giggled. "He would stress out too much to remember!"

"I've had another idea, too. Grab your pad and come in my office. We need to publish another article in the paper and see if we can't generate some leads."

Amanda followed with her pad in her hand.

§

"Hey, Barney," Joshua Finley said, reaching his hand out. "Can I borrow your phone for a minute?"

"What's wrong with yours?"

"I don't know where it is." Josh patted his front and back jeans pockets.

"Ha! I bet it's in the dumpster!" Cyrus McDaniel called out from across the room. "I heard a phone ringing in there this morning."

"There's a phone ringing in the dumpster?" Cody Beck said as he tossed a wood scrap in the trash pile.

"What? No, that can't be mine. I had mine at lunch, but now I can't find it."

"What were you doing in the dumpster?" Cody Beck said, laughing at Cyrus.

"Well here," Max Alvarez said. "Let me call your phone. Maybe you'll hear it ring." Max Alvarez pulled his phone off the clip from the back of his belt and scrolled through his contacts.

"I don't know if that will work. I think the ringer might be turned off."

"Oh?" Max said with a snicker. "You got lady troubles?"

"Yeah, Melody's mad at me and she's been calling and texting. After she yelled at me this morning, I think I turned my ringer off."

"Melody?" Max said. "I thought it was Sandy."

"No, this morning it was Melody that called me."

"Didn't you just tell me you were dating Sandy Teague?"

"Yeah," Josh said. "Sometimes."

"Uh oh. So, you're dating both of them?" Max said.

"Sometimes," Josh said.

"Well, that's why they're blowing up your phone," Cody Beck yelled, and Cyrus McDaniel held up his hand to quiet him. Max held out his phone to show the display said it was calling Josh's phone, but Josh didn't hear anything.

"I guess I do have the ringer off. It's in here somewhere."

"Are you sure?" Max said as he canceled the call and put his phone back into his belt.

"I'm sure." Josh barked. "Barney, let me use your phone."

Joe Barney turned his back on Josh. "I don't need those women having my number! They'll be calling me trying to find out where you are."

Josh reached toward Max Alvarez with an open hand. "Max?"

"You're not getting mine, either. My wife will kill me if your women start calling."

"Come on guys," Josh whined.

Cy McDaniels laughed and pointed downstairs. "Try the dumpster."

Josh stomped off and huffed as all the guys laughed.

§

"That's a little... uh..."

"What, Connie?" Cora rolled her eyes at the phone in her hand.

"Unorthodox," Conrad said carefully. "There could be some repercussions."

"Such as?"

"Well, it could just heighten gossip and produce a lot of bad information. Everyone wants to give their two cents—" Conrad spoke slowly and stammered, trying to think and speak at the same time. His hesitation was a sign of indecision that Cora could exploit.

"It could also answer questions about whether he made it to the demolition derby or whether he drove his own truck out of town. It's possible he was there all evening and we just haven't found that witness. That's several hours of time unaccounted for."

"Well, go ahead and run your article. I guess it's okay. I want to know what it says before it's printed, though. I think it's just going to put everybody in a whirlwind. There are too many busybodies in town, and we'll get a hundred crazy reports to wade through."

"Yes, but you might get one good thing out of it after spending hours reading all the crazy stuff." Cora saw Amanda at her door with a piece of paper in her hand and crooked her index finger for Amanda to come in.

"We need some kind of lead. We have no clues how he got from the construction site to where his truck was found. Yeah. Yeah, okay. I agree. Go ahead and give it a try, but I don't know when we'll have time to read them all."

"I asked Amanda to add an email link and she may be able to weed some of them out for you. If they're not about Owen or if they're not about Friday or Saturday, she won't forward them to Wink. That could reduce some of the reports. I don't want to put the responsibility on her shoulders to be the only one looking, but I know it's going to be time-consuming."

"I've got Wink out interviewing. He's canvassing the area. He's got a whole list of people to see. It may even be a list you made. He's going to talk to everybody that lives on North Road and see if anyone saw anything. Then he's going to the pit crews and the garages connected to the derby. Unless he was hiding somewhere, he must have run into somebody Friday night."

"Wink is a man that recognizes the value of a good list," Cora said, smiling. "I hate to say this, but we need to know more than when he was last seen. We need…"

"A body?" Conrad offered. "I know."

"I'm hoping since one hasn't turned up, that it means he's alive and just not in Spicetown," Cora said.

"I hope you're right."

§

Marking names off his list, Wink dialed the phone number for the union representative. "Mr. Dooley? I'm Officer Harold Hobson of the Spicetown Police Department."

"Good afternoon, Officer. I'm Parnell Dooley. How can I help you?"

"I have a few questions regarding your union member, Owen Hollingsworth. I'm told that you have been advised of his failure to show up for work Monday?"

"Certainly, Officer. His wife called Monday morning and told me that he had not come home from work on Friday and that she had reported it to the police."

"Yes, sir. Can you tell me the last time you saw Mr. Hollingsworth?"

"Well, it's been a few weeks. He had a situation at work, a meeting with his supervisor, and I was invited to attend."

"So, you didn't see him last week at all? Did you hear from him? Maybe he called?"

"No, sir."

"And how did the meeting go with the supervisor?" Wink asked.

"It was fine. There was some equipment missing, but it was a misunderstanding. His supervisor thought he had signed out the equipment, but he hadn't, so there was no disciplinary action."

"Oh?"

"No, just a discussion. I was there as representation because Mr. Hollingsworth is a long-time union member. He wasn't involved."

"Well, if you hear from him or think of anything that might be relevant, please call the Spicetown Police Department."

"I certainly will, Officer. We want to help in any way that we can."

"Appreciate it," Wink said.

The call disconnected and Parnell looked up. "Are you sure this is the right thing to do? Maybe we should tell the police."

"If I thought it had anything to do with his disappearance, I would agree with you, but it doesn't."

"I guess not. I just, I guess I just lied to the police, and I'm uncomfortable with that." Parnell wiped perspiration from his brow.

"You didn't lie. You haven't seen him in over a week. You don't know where he is."

"I know, but you know what I mean. I'm not telling them everything." Parnell lowered his head.

"You've told them all they need to know."

CHAPTER 16

Cora Mae stood on the front steps with one shoulder holding open the screen door as she lifted the door knocker on Owen Hollingsworth's front door. The door opened slowly to a tiny woman with tinted wire framed glasses. The face was familiar, but Cora couldn't recall from where.

"Good morning, Mrs. Hollingsworth. My name is Cora Mae Bingham. I'm the mayor of Spicetown. I don't believe we've met, but I was hoping I could talk to you for a moment."

"Oh, yes, Mayor. I know who you are. I'm sorry. Please, come in. Have a seat. Can I get you anything?

"No ma'am. I'm sorry we're meeting at such a bad time, but we are working on finding your husband."

"I'm so grateful for your help. I don't know what else to do. I've called everyone I know."

"I understand, Mrs. Hollingsworth. I know this must be a scary time for you."

"Please, call me Bonita. I want you to know that Owen would never do this. I know people want to believe that he's run away, but that's just not possible. Owen would not do that. He's lived here his whole life. He has friends and family here, and he wouldn't leave me. We've been married for 23 years and we have a good marriage."

"I understand. I came by because I would like to put an article in the newspaper today asking if anyone has seen your husband. Maybe at the Demolition derby Friday night or anywhere after Friday at 5:00 o'clock when he left work. I was hoping you had a good picture that I could put in the paper. Maybe someone saw him that didn't know his name. We are trying to figure out where he went when he left work. Someone in town may have clues that we can use."

"Oh yes ma'am. I sure do. That's a great idea. I have family pictures and we had a picture taken together last year. He's all dressed up in a suit. He looks really nice. You can cut me out of it." Bonita bustled off to the back of the house holding up her finger to indicate it would take her a minute to locate the photo. Cora looked around the living room and into the kitchen. It was a working kitchen. It was clean, with plates drying in the dish drainer and appliances pulled out with a dishcloth tossed on the counter. The kitchen looked like the center of the home. She expected Bonita spent most of her time there. The newspaper, The Spicetown Star, was on the dining room table with a cup of coffee beside it.

"Here you go," Bonita said. "I brought a few others. This was taken on Owen's birthday a few months ago. We had some of his friends over and we barbecued in the backyard." Cora glanced down at the photo and saw Owen Hollingsworth holding up his hand to wave and standing beside a charcoal grill. His friend and coworker, Joe Barney, stood on the other side of the grill with a smile on his face and a hot dog bun in his hand.

"Joe Barney," Cora said, tapping her finger on the picture.

"Yes, you know Joe?" Bonita said, as she lowered her tiny frame to the couch beside Cora. "Owen calls him Barney, but I call him Joe."

"I do. I met your husband recently. He has been working on the community center."

"Oh, yes," Bonita said nodding with a proud smile. "He told me that you stop by and see him every day."

"I like to check on things."

"He says you are a good mayor."

Cora smiled as Bonita leaned over the pictures. "This one," Bonita said, pointing to the professional photo of the couple, "This one is a nice picture of Owen, but really for people trying to recognize him, he usually looks like that." She pointed to the party picnic photos and gave Cora a sad smile. "He didn't dress up very often, but I think he cleaned up really well." The heartbreak in Bonita's eyes opened wounds in Cora's heart and she patted Bonita's hand. Missing someone was a special sadness only understood by those who have suffered an unacceptable loss.

"These will both do very well. Thank you, Bonita. We'll make some copies and get these originals back to you soon. I want you to know we're doing all that we can, and you call us if you need anything," Cora said standing. "Officer Hobson will keep you updated, but I've got to rush back to City Hall right now. I want to get this in the paper tonight."

Bonita opened the front door for Cora. "Thank you."

Cora waved as she hurried down the steps to her car.

§

"Hey, Wink," Georgia Marks said, holding her hand up in the air and waving a green message slip. "The Chief called."

Wink nodded as he walked up and snatched the telephone message from Georgia's hand and turned to glance over his shoulder when the guys in the office began to snicker. Glancing at the message slip he knew why.

"You gonna give her a call, Wink?" Tabor asked. "Chief says she's got all the answers."

Wink stared at the message. *Return call to Phoebe Louise.*

"Maybe I'll assign that task to you, Tabor," Wink said. "You can give the psychic a call and see if she knows where Hollingsworth is hiding, since you can't find him."

"That's right," Asher said. "Delegate."

"I'm happy to give her a call. Maybe she'll read my palm and tell me I'm going to win the lottery." Tabor held open his hand and peered at the lines.

"I don't think she does that," Asher said. "She just grabs your arm and hums and looks off into space."

Wink chuckled when Officer Roy Asher grabbed Officer Tabor's arm and imitated Phoebe Louise receiving a psychic vision.

"Hey, she helped you find your dog, didn't she?" Tabor said to Wink after shaking Asher's hand from his forearm. "Didn't she tell you that you would meet someone and form a great friendship right before you got Hank?"

"Yeah," Wink said. "But I don't think that qualifies her for police work."

"Well, she must be getting some vibes about Owen Hollingsworth. She hasn't called the PD in a while." Tabor hunched his shoulder in a dismissive shrug.

"Didn't you date her once?" Asher blurted out and Tabor laughed.

Georgia hung up the phone and pushed her chair to the opening of the dispatch booth.

"I'll go ahead and give her a call if you want. It can't hurt anything. She's actually a very nice lady. I don't know if there's anything to it, but she believes in it. She means well," Georgia said as she took the message slip that Wink handed to her and pushed her chair back into the booth. Wink looked at Tabor and Asher in a shared rebuke.

Wink walked back to the Chief's office and pulled out the chair. The desktop was littered with phone messages that had come in during the night shift. Some of them we're just nosy inquiries, but others were trying to offer information. One of them caught his eye and he picked it up. It was from a woman who said she was Joshua Finley's girlfriend. Her message said that Joshua was supposed to come to her house Friday night, but he never showed up. Wink pushed that message to the side. He recalled Cora's notes saying Joshua had a date Friday night, but he hadn't followed up with the woman he went out with. Maybe Finley was not telling the truth about his whereabouts.

§

"Mayor?" Amanda spoke softly as she leaned around Cora's office door. "Miss Hollingsworth is here to see you. She's paying her water bill right now, but says she'd like to see you if you have a minute."

Cora nodded as Amanda shrugged in apology.

Moments later, Ruth Hollingsworth was standing at Cora's doorway holding her purse in both hands at her waist. "Hello, Ruth. Come on in."

"I'm sorry to come without an appointment, Cora, but I was hoping you could tell me if anything is being done about my brother."

"Of course, Ruth. They are working on tracing Owen's steps on Friday night. They've been interviewing for days. You know his truck was found."

"I do," Ruth said clutching her purse and straightening her back. "His wife is worried to death. She's not very bright, you know. She's sweet, but she's not very bright." Ruth winced. "Bless her heart. I just don't know what to tell her."

"I understand. It must be very stressful for you both."

"It may be that Owen up and left. Who knows what happens behind closed doors?"

"Was Owen unhappy with his life?"

"I don't think so," Ruth said, glancing around the room. "I thought he was satisfied with his marriage and his work choice. He has a number of friends."

"Well, if you think of anything, remember anything he has said or—"

"Oh, no. I haven't spoken with Owen in months myself. His wife has called, of course. I think she's called everyone in town, but I have no idea what Owen does from day to day."

"Well, when you speak to his wife again, please assure her that we are doing everything that we can."

"Thank you," Ruth said turning to leave. "Oh, Cora. Is this going to change anything with the community center? Will this delay your construction work?"

"No, Ruth. I don't expect it to."

"That's good to hear," Ruth said as her posture relaxed.

"Have a good day," Cora said as she walked around her desk to help escort Ruth through her door and across Amanda's office to the lobby.

Amanda looked up with round eyes as Cora watched Ruth leave through the lobby doors.

"Did you hear what she said?" Cora said as she walked to Amanda's desk. "She asked if Owen's disappearance was going to delay the community center construction. She's concerned about whether she's going to get to book the community center for her book sale event. She hasn't even spoken to her brother in months."

"Well, some siblings are not close," Amanda said sheepishly.

"Perhaps," Cora huffed. "I don't have any, but if I did, I definitely would keep an eye on them."

Amanda nodded with a mischievous smirk.

"Just like I do everyone else." Cora returned to her office with a chuckle.

CHAPTER 17

"Oh, my aching feet," Cora said as she slipped off the offending shoes and lifted her legs to stretch to the ottoman. Marmalade was already curled up on the overstuffed footstool and they both had just eaten dinner.

"I should throw these shoes away," Cora said holding one in the air to show Marmalade. "They make me miserable every time I wear them."

Marmalade stared at Cora with a mixture of cat apathy and curiosity.

"You're lucky you don't wear shoes," Cora said as her phone rang in the kitchen. Groaning, she pushed herself out of the chair and rushed to get the phone.

"Hey, Connie." Cora answered with a breathy sigh.

"You sound out of breath. Is everything okay?"

"Yes, sorry. I left my phone in my purse, so I had to jog to the kitchen. You know what an athlete I am," Cora laughed.

"See, you had your exercise for the evening. I'm glad I could help." Conrad chuckled.

"Walking to the construction site every morning has been good for me, too. I should really find time to do more of that. Has anything new turned up?"

"Wink is working on things."

"The article ran in tonight's paper, so maybe we'll get something from it tomorrow. I talked to Owen's sister, Ruth, today and his wife, Bonita. I didn't learn anything new from them though."

"Cora, you don't have to investigate."

Cora settled back into her favorite armchair again. "I'm not investigating."

"Well, that's what it sounds like."

"No. Not at all. I'm just asking questions."

Conrad's laughter startled Cora and she pulled the phone away from her ear. "What do you think investigating is?"

"Well, you know what I mean."

"Wink is working on this. You can trust him.

"I know. I'm not doing anything differently. If you were here, I'd be doing the same thing."

Conrad chuckled again. "I know. You don't think I can do my job either."

"Now, I don't want either of you to take it that way. I don't nose around and ask questions because I doubt your ability or Wink's. I'm trying to help. I have different kinds of contacts than you do, but this issue is as important to me as it is to the police. Owen Hollingsworth is a citizen of Spicetown, and I keep an eye on the citizens of Spicetown, just in a different way than you do."

"I know you do."

"Now," Cora said tossing her legs back on the ottoman beside Marmalade. "Did you talk to Wink tonight? Did he learn anything from the garage? He said he was going out there to see if Owen showed up for pit crew on Friday night."

"I talked to him, but he still hasn't found anybody that saw him. The problem is, none of them were concerned when he didn't show up."

"Right now, it looks like Owen left work Friday night and Alan Avery was the last person to see him. I just can't believe that Alan has anything to do with this. He was frustrated with Owen. I knew that."

"How did you know that? Had he talked to you about him before he disappeared?"

"I heard Alan talking to Erika. I know he was frustrated that Owen was messing up at work."

"They talked about Owen to you?"

"Not exactly. I just overheard them talking."

"You were eavesdropping."

"Kind of," Cora said, rolling her eyes.

"So, maybe there is something to the fact that Avery was out to get Hollingsworth."

"No. Don't be silly. Are you implying Alan did something to Owen? You think he paid Owen off to run away from home?"

"It's possible that their last discussion wasn't as friendly as he indicated. There is no witness. Maybe there was a fight."

"You're not suggesting Alan Avery killed Owen Hollingsworth?" Cora shrieked.

"It's possible."

"No," Cora said, shaking her head in disgust.

"Cora, just because you knew him when he was ten years old doesn't mean he's not capable of any wrongdoing. Anyone can kill."

"I know Alan Avery isn't killing anybody. If there was a fight, it was with words."

"Let me guess," Conrad said clearing his throat. "Alan was a student of yours and he never got in a fight."

"He didn't throw a punch as a little boy and I know he wouldn't do it now."

"Okay, tell me a little more about Alan Avery. Is he married?"

"No. He went away to college and I heard he had a fiancée, but something happened, and they never married. He's actually living outside of town now, about two miles east of town in that nice little blue house with the white shutters. He built it himself when he was just starting in construction. It took him a couple of years to get it done."

"There used to be an old green trailer sitting out there. Is that the house?"

"Yes, he lived in the trailer while he worked on the house. I think he has a business degree, so I'm not sure how he got into construction."

"What do you know about Erika Johnson?" Conrad asked.

"She's a sweet girl. I don't know much about her personal life. She has a husband and 2 sons. She's mentioned them to me. She lives in Paxton and used to work for a different construction company. That's all I know."

"Did she share the same feelings about Owen that Avery had?"

"She didn't say anything bad about Owen to me."

"What about when you were eavesdropping?"

"I wasn't, no. She just let Alan vent. He was upset that day. She didn't really agree or disagree."

"People get frustrated in their jobs, Cora. If they take their work seriously, things can get heated. Wink is looking hard into that."

"I can see a shouting match, maybe. But I can't see Alan being physically aggressive."

"It might have been Hollingsworth," Conrad said. "He may have lashed out at Avery and Avery defended himself."

"Pfft. I don't see it."

"So, what do you think happened to Owen?" Conrad said.

"I wish I knew," Cora said. "Finding the truck, it just doesn't give me a good feeling."

"You mean you think something bad happened?"

"I do. If the truck hadn't been found, I might still be able to hold on to the belief that he ran away, he left his wife, left the town, left his family, but with the truck abandoned, I think something bad happened to him."

"I've been thinking the same thing. I've talked to Wink about it. I think maybe we need to be looking for a body as much as we are interviewing for a location where he was last seen. We don't have the manpower we need to search the whole field, but I told Wink to put a couple of guys out on that leased land and have them search wider. They searched around the truck before it was towed to town to be printed and inventoried, but they haven't really looked in the cornfields. It's close to harvest time. If he's in those fields, we don't want the combine to find him."

"Oh my, no," Cora said, shuddering at the gruesome thought of a body turning up in a combine harvester. "Maybe the community could help with a search. Who leases that land? The workers need to know."

"Wink talked to them and told them to report anything they find unusual. They will keep their eyes open. I'd just like to find it before they do."

"Yes," Cora said with a sigh. "So how did Briscoe do? Did he scale the wall and find the man in the warehouse?"

"He ran right up that wall. No problem at all. He was a little skittish coming down though," Conrad said.

"I guess it's just like a ladder to him. It's easier to go up."

"The warehouse was a little intimidating the first time. I don't think he knew why he was in there. He sniffed around a little bit and then came out looking for me. I think he thought I should be in there, too. The trainer said he just needs to learn some search commands. A slow start, but he did find the guy, so he passed the test." Conrad said. "I almost think he was trained by somebody. He's too good at this stuff."

"He might have been a working dog. We don't know where he came from."

"But why would somebody dump a dog this smart, this capable, especially if they spent time training him?"

"I can't explain that. People do it every day, dogs and cats, and I'm baffled." Cora said. "You know Marmalade came from the city shelter. Someone left her there as a kitten."

"Well, I think we're coming home this weekend."

"That's great news."

"They're running out of things to test him on and he's passing everything, so I think they'll give him a certificate Saturday and send us home."

"I'm sure Wink will be grateful. Your absence is ruining his love life." Cora laughed. "Every time he tries to have a date, it gets interrupted."

"Am I supposed to feel bad about that?" Conrad said.

"Oh, Connie," Cora scolded and laughed.

§

"Good morning," Bryan Stotlar said as his head peeked around the door to Amanda's office.

"Hi! What brings you to town this morning?"

"I had to run some herbs over to the Old Thyme Italian Restaurant and so I stopped off at the Fennel Street Bakery." Bryan placed a small white sack in front of Amanda. "I thought I'd get you some breakfast."

"Oh, thank you. What is it?"

"It's a bear claw. Isn't that your favorite?"

"It is! I haven't had one of these in a long time."

"I thought maybe we could have dinner tonight. You can come out to the house and I'll cook."

"Sounds like a great idea," Amanda said, smiling as she flattened the white sack into a plate for her bear claw.

"Do you want some coffee?"

"No, thanks. I've got some in the truck. Is the mayor in yet?"

"No, but I expect her any minute. Have you talked to the police yet about the guy on the road?"

"No, I haven't. I was going to tell the mayor and see if she thinks I should go down there. I could stop by the PD before I go back to the house."

"Good morning," Cora said with a lyrical cheer as she came in the door with her handbag over her arm. "There's a chill in the air today."

"Yes, ma'am," Bryan said. "Autumn is coming."

"Good morning, Mayor. Bryan stopped by and wanted to ask you about the man he saw on North Road."

"Oh, yes. Amanda told me that you saw someone walking."

"I did. I saw somebody walking down the road Friday night. It was dark. Not pitch dark, but dusk, so—"

"You could tell it was a man?"

"Oh, yeah."

"Was there anything in his hand, like a gas can or a bag or anything?" Cora asked.

"No. I don't remember him holding anything. I couldn't see him real well, but I—"

"Could you tell what clothing he had on? What color?"

"I probably could have, but I can't remember. I didn't really pay close attention."

"I understand," Cora said. "You didn't know him though?"

"No," Bryan said as he slumped.

"He doesn't know Owen Hollingsworth, though," Amanda said. "Here. I still have his wife's pictures." Amanda shuffled papers around on her desk to find the photos Bonita Hollingsworth had shared with Cora.

"Old? Young?" Cora said with raised eyebrows.

"Somewhere in between," Bryan said with a question in his tone. "I would say older than me, but not old."

"Hair color?"

"Ugh," Bryan slouched more. "Brownish? I mean he wasn't blonde or white headed."

"Okay," Cora nodded. "Tall or short? Heavy or thin?"

"Not extraordinarily either one," Bryan said. "Just a guy, a regular looking guy."

"Well, I would say that it wasn't Owen Hollingsworth then." Cora nodded curtly.

Amanda set up straight. "You're sure?"

"I wouldn't describe Owen as a regular looking guy," Cora said. "He's extremely tall and thin, maybe six foot two or three and less than two hundred pounds."

"Oh, well then," Bryan took a deep breath. "I don't think I saw him."

"Here," Amanda held up the photos. "I found them."

"You can't really see his height or body shape in these, but—"

"That could be him," Bryan pointed. "He looked kind of like that guy." Bryan stabbed his finger at the picture.

Amanda jumped out of her chair to peer over Bryan's shoulder. "That's not Owen. This guy is Owen. That's Joe Barney, his friend."

"Hmm," Cora said with a frown.

"Oh, I'm not saying it was that guy exactly. I couldn't swear to it, but it could be."

"Even if he wasn't Owen, Wink still needs to know about him," Cora said. "If we could find him, someone walking on the road would have noticed the cars passing him better than another driver. He might have seen something."

"That's true," Amanda said. "When I'm walking in the neighborhood, I notice the cars and the people in them, but when I'm driving, I rarely look that close. You don't get to see them very long when you pass in a car."

"I'm going to see Wink shortly because I'm going to stop by the Police Department after I go to the construction site. I'll tell him what you've told me. He may call you if he has more questions. He's been doing a lot of questioning up and down your road."

"Wait," Amanda said, throwing her hands out to the side. "My dad saw Joe Barney. I'm sure he told me he passed him on North Road when he was coming home from the Beck's Farm. I can't remember if it was Friday night or Saturday night."

"Joe was walking?" Cora asked.

"No. Dad said he passed him driving and waved. He brings his dogs to dad's office."

"Have you asked your mom if she's heard anything down at the shop? I know everyone talks pretty freely down there and there's quite a bit of—"

"Idle gossip?" Amanda said, laughing.

"Well," Cora said. "Just stories from different people.

"Not that I can think of," Amanda said. "I can ask her."

"Maybe I need to get my hair done," Cora said, patting her hair with the palm of her hand. "Call her and see if she can work me in."

Amanda giggled as Cora winked at her.

CHAPTER 18

Pulling over to park near the curb, Cora grabbed her umbrella and slid it into her large handbag before heading towards the trailer. It was too chilly to walk today, and she could smell rain in the air. The morning commotion on the work site amused her and she looked around when she heard men's voices barking orders from one side to the other. Backhoes were working in the parking lot and a delivery truck pulled near the back of the building to unload supplies. Trucks backing up were beeping and saws were buzzing as Cora Mae knocked on the trailer door.

"Good morning, Mrs. B." Alan Avery motioned for Cora to enter.

"How are you today?"

"So far so good," Alan said. "You just missed Erika. She's around back, checking on the delivery truck."

"It is very active this morning. Did all the welding get done yesterday?"

"Unfortunately, no. Cheryl is going to come back on Friday and finish up. She's booked for the next couple of days. It will be ready for her when she comes," Alan said as he pulled out the chair behind his desk.

"What's going on in the parking lot today?" Cora had parked on the side because she saw Sammy Lowe and Grant LeMasters working in the parking lot.

"The finishing is scheduled for Friday, so the guys are digging the front ditch a little deeper to make sure it'll handle any runoff from rain or melting snow. We wanted to wait until the last of the deliveries were complete before we finished the lot. We're getting close to the end. The glass still has to be set, but next week we'll be moving inside to work on finishing touches. There's still some work to do on the main floor and some details in the offices. Have you been upstairs since the sheet rock was finished? The offices on the east side are ready for paint."

"Well, you timed it just right because it's trying to get cold."

"I see that," Alan chuckled. "Before you leave today, try to grab Erika. She has the paint samples and needs you to confirm the colors before she orders."

Cora pushed open the trailer's door. "I'll find her."

"Avery! Where is Avery?" Cody Beck was screaming at the guy standing on the West side of building and Cora looked over her shoulder.

"Alan, Cody needs you."

Alan followed Cora down the trailer steps and raised his hand to wave towards Cody.

Cody waved back and began running towards them. "You need to come over here right now," Cody took a deep breath. "Sorry, Mayor. Good morning."

"Good morning," Cora said and stepped aside so Cody could talk to Alan.

"The trash truck," Cody said pointing to the side alley. "The driver, he needs to talk to you."

"What's the matter?" Alan frowned at him. Cody's face was flushed, and his words were edged with panic.

"The truck driver." Cody's head turned to the alley as he pointed again. "There's a problem. He needs a supervisor. I don't know for sure, but I think," Cody looked hesitantly at Cora. "I think there's somebody in the dumpster."

"Somebody in the dumpster? Excuse me, Mrs. B." Alan began to run towards the side alley where the truck was idling. Cora Mae bustled behind him, trying not to draw attention to herself.

"I'm Alan Avery, the site supervisor. Can I help you?" Alan stepped back as the driver climbed from the truck.

"Yeah, I just got off the phone with my supervisor. He told me to stop the truck and he called the police. It looks like there's somebody in my hopper." The driver looked to his left and then his right. "My hopper has a camera and I'm pretty sure I saw somebody."

"We need to get them out." Alan said as he put his hands on his hips. "How do you get in this thing? They might be hurt." Cora leaned in closer behind Alan to hear.

"It looks like a hand. There's a hand sticking up and that guy over there said he thought he saw a body fall in when I turned the dumpster up. Maybe it's nothing. Maybe it's fake. I've had people put stuff in the dumpster just to try to freak me out, but I can't take no chances."

"Definitely not," Alan agreed.

"I have to wait for the police. That's procedure." The driver climbed back up in his truck but left his door open.

Cora reached into her bag and pulled out her phone. "Let me call and make sure somebody's on their way." A police car pulled into the alley before Georgia Marks had a chance to answer the phone. "Never mind, Georgie. It's just Cora Bingham. I was calling to see if someone was on their way to the construction site, but I see—"

"Yes, ma'am. He just got there, and Wink is coming down, too."

"Thank you. Georgie." Cora hung up the phone and greeted Roy Asher.

"Morning, Mayor," Officer Asher said as he approached Cora and turned to Alan. "I'm Officer Asher. How can I help?"

"I'm Alan Avery. I'm the site supervisor here and this gentleman thinks he saw something fall from our trash dumpster."

Roy nodded and walked to the open truck door.

"If you jump up here in the truck, I can show you," the driver said. "We got a camera back there." Roy went around the truck and after two or three tries was able to hoist himself into the passenger seat. Cora and Alan waited for Roy Asher to return.

"I agree," Roy said to Alan as he walked back around the truck. "It needs a second look. Could you get your workers to move away from the truck?" Cora looked up and saw that a dozen or more construction workers stood around in a semicircle.

"Come on, guys. Get back to work." Alan waved his arms as the onlookers dispersed with a scowl.

"I think we need to talk to Wink," Cora said, just as she felt the first raindrop hit the back of her hand. "He's on his way."

Roy nodded and stepped away to radio dispatch from his car. When Wink pulled in behind him, Cora tried to wait patiently for Roy to update him, but the weather was concerning her.

"Wink, it's starting to rain, and I think you're going to have to look through the contents. Maybe we should call Alice at the coroner's office. See what she recommends." Wink shifted his weight from one foot to another and looked at his phone. Cora sensed that he wanted to call Conrad. "If you need somewhere to dump the contents, you could take it out to the city garage and have the truck empty it there." Cora paused and studied Wink's face as a quick decision was needed. "Would you like me to call Alice?" Cora said as she pushed open her umbrella.

Wink's eyes were searching for answers and Cora expected his heart was beating loudly. "Yes, Mayor. Please call Coroner Warner and see what she would like us to do. I'm going to speak with the driver's supervisor. Find out how many stops he made before here."

"Good idea," Cora said, trying to bolster Wink's confidence as she punched the number in her phone to call Alice Warner.

§

"Alice is on her way." Cora nodded at Wink. "She's going to meet us at the city shed. She said it was okay to have the truck moved there if it has all the contents of the dumpster."

Wink shuffled his feet. "I'm just waiting for him to get done talking to his supervisor. He said he'd send somebody to pick up the driver, but we need to take the truck and keep the dumpster for now. I guess I should call the Chief." Wink looked down at his feet nervously.

"We probably need to get all these people away from this area. I suppose you need to, you know, look around here for clues."

"Yeah. Yeah," Wink said. "We need to get everybody back and put up some tape."

"I can talk to Erika and Alan for you, if you'd like to give Conrad a call."

"Okay, yeah, that will help. Thank you, Mayor."

Cora walked up to Alan and Erika standing on the side with a group of onlookers. Although Alan had told them to get back to work, somehow, they seem to regather when he turned around.

"So? What's up, Mrs. B? What are they gonna do?" Alan stood with his arms folded across his chest and his feet planted.

"They're going to take the dumpster, and they will need to have this area cleared of people."

"Yeah, yeah. I understand, but we're going to need another dumpster."

"You can call the company and see about setting one up somewhere else maybe, while they're working, but this area needs to stay clear for the police to go over. They'll be putting up some tape and we need to keep the workers out of this area."

"Gotcha," Alan said.

Erika reached out a hand for Cora's arm. "There is somebody in there?"

Cora nodded her head sadly. "There appears to be, but we don't know anything more than that right now. They're going to take the truck and check things out. How often does the trash get picked up here?"

Alan looked over Cora's head in thought. "Every week. I have called them before to come when it's been full, but usually this time every week."

Cora hummed. There's no telling how many days had passed, and now that the contents had been dumped into the truck it would be harder to tell how far down in the dumpster the body had been. "I think maybe after the truck leaves you can call and have them bring out another dumpster."

"We'll take care of that," Erika said.

"Yeah," Alan said. "Let me see if I can get these guys back to work." Alan walked off towards the crowd and began making waving motions with his arms, pushing back the crowd and shouting orders that they needed to get back to their assignments again.

Erika remained beside Cora. "I don't know what to say, Mayor. This job has had so many problems."

"Oh, don't say that."

"Strange, horrible things keep happening. I just can't imagine that there's a body in there. How horrible, what a horrible way to go. I can't imagine what happened to him."

"The coroner will hopefully be able to tell the story behind that. It's their job."

"You don't think it's Owen Hollingsworth, do you?"

"There's no way to know that, dear," Cora said. "Is there some reason you would think it might be Owen?"

"Oh, no. I thought he just took off," Erika said, shrugging her shoulders. "I never thought that anything bad happened to him. Even when his truck was found, I just thought he had gone off with another woman. You know how men are," Erika huffed.

"Well, it's a mystery," Cora said, "And I know they're still working on that, too. Don't you let this trouble you. They'll try to take care of the area and get everything back to normal as soon as possible. I'm sure."

"Please let me know what they find out," Erika said, squeezing Cora Mae's hand in hers.

"I will, dear. Don't worry."

Erika turned to go back to the trailer and Cora walked back to her car to call Jimmy Kole. She needed to warn him there would be a lot of trash coming his way soon at the city garage.

§

"Chief, we got a situation," Wink said under his breath. "There was a dead body in a dumpster at the construction site."

"You need to remove that dumpster and all the contents—". Conrad covered his mouth and turned his head. He and Briscoe were waiting for the trainers to set up the area for the next class.

"He's not in the dumpster now," Wink said.

"You moved him?" Conrad blurted out and jumped up when he saw all the eyes in the room were on him. Nodding an apology to the others, he walked away from the seating area.

"No, they found him when they came to empty the dumpster," Wink said.

"So where is the body now?" Conrad said in a softer tone as he walked to stand near the door to the class.

"Out at the city garage. The mayor said we could use the shed area to empty the trash truck and go through it. It's raining here and we needed cover."

Conrad took a deep breath and released some tension. "So, the body was in the back of the trash truck before it was discovered?"

"Yeah, Chief. The driver saw it and had somebody call us."

Conrad ran his hand over the top of his head. *Why didn't any of his officers start their stories at the beginning?* "Okay, so you had the driver go to the shed and dump the contents, right? Did you call the coroner's office?"

"The mayor did, while I was talking to the driver's supervisor. The coroner is here now."

"Is it Hollingsworth?" Conrad's jaw flexed awaiting the answer.

"Yep, Asher said it's him," Wink said. "He's got identification on him, but he's pretty messed up. He's got a serious head wound."

"Has Alice said anything yet?"

"No, she's still looking at him," Wink said, glancing over at Coroner Alice Warner, who was bent over the body.

"Is that your Chief?" Alice barked as she looked up.

Wink nodded.

Alice yanked off her glove and held out her hand. "Let me talk to him."

Wink handed his phone to her and crossed his arms over his chest.

"Connie?"

"Hey, Alice," Conrad said. "Have you got any idea what happened?"

"Blunt force trauma to the head," Alice said as she stepped over the body. "No doubt about that, but until we clean him up, I can't tell you much more."

"How long? The guy's been missing since Friday night."

"Yep," Alice said. "The best I can do right now is to say I would place time of death more than thirty-six hours ago."

"Okay, Alice. I'll be back in town soon. Keep us posted."

"Will do," Alice said as she thrust the phone back at Wink.

"Thirty-six hours?" Wink said as Alice put a clean glove on her right hand. "How can you tell?"

"Cold, but not stiff," Alice said, waving to the ambulance backing up to urge them on.

"Any idea about the head wound? Can you tell what type of object hit him?" Wink couldn't look closely at the side of Owen's head and preserve his dignity. He preferred dealing with the living.

"Can't say without cleaning," Alice said as the ambulance pulled out a stretcher. "It may be the side of the dumpster. Did you see it?" Alice walked over to the dumpster. The truck had dropped it near the opening of the next garage bay.

Wink followed reluctantly.

"See?" Alice pointed to the inside of the dumpster and Wink held his flashlight up on the area.

"Dried blood." Wink quickly scanned the bottom of the dumpster with his light before stepping back to hold his breath.

"Brain matter. Too early to say for sure," Alice said walking back to the ambulance. "I'll let you know as soon as I do."

Wink had seen the coroner's office staff take photos of the dumpster and had urged Asher to do the same. The scene may be easier to examine from photos because the odor was distorting his thought processes.

"You've got to bag everything," Wink said when Asher walked up.

"Everything?" Asher said throwing back his shoulders. "Where are we going to put all this stuff?"

"We're going to send everything with dried blood on it to the lab. We need to sort it out."

"This is going to take all day," Asher sighed.

§

"Listen," Conrad said as he crouched down. "We need to get home, buddy. Were you paying attention? You need to do just what he tells you and get through this test."

Briscoe stared into Conrad's eyes with what seemed like full understanding.

"Can you do that?" Conrad stroked Briscoe's cheek and rubbed his neck. "If we don't get home soon, Cora Mae is going to dive in that dumpster herself."

Conrad smiled and put his hands on his knees to stand up. "Let's go."

CHAPTER 19

"Hey, honey," Bryan said when Amanda answered the phone. "Are you busy?"

"Hi! No, the mayor isn't here right now. I thought you were working out back today. Did you get rained out?"

"No, I moved to the greenhouse, but it's pouring rain out there now. I've got plenty to do in here."

"Is Mavis working the front?"

"Yeah, that's why I called. She told me about the body in the dumpster. Everybody says it's that Owen guy. Is that true?"

"What body in the dumpster?" Amanda scowled and glanced up as Cora Mae walked through the door.

"They found a guy dead in the dumpster this morning at the construction site. You didn't know?"

"No! How did Mavis hear this?"

"She went in Chervil Drugs this morning to pick up her check and somebody there told her," Bryan said.

"The mayor just walked in. I need to make sure she knows. I'll call you back."

Amanda ran around the side of her desk to Cora's doorway. "Mayor? Bryan just told me that they found a body in the dumpster at the construction site this morning and it may be Owen Hollingsworth. Is that true?"

"My goodness," Cora Mae said leaning back in her office chair and kicking off her shoes under her desk. "Word does travel fast. Bryan's not even in town."

"It is true," Amanda said with wide eyes. "That's awful. His poor wife."

"I hope Wink can tell her before someone else in town does. With the way gossip races around here, he better hurry."

"I am starting to get some replies to the newspaper article you did," Amanda said. "Nothing that seems relevant yet, but we've had some replies."

"That's good, dear. You keep an eye on it. Conrad told me that Briscoe is doing really well, and he hopes to be home this weekend. Until then, we'll need to do what we can to help Wink."

"I asked my mom last night if she'd heard anything, but all I got back is a lot of hearsay. I'm not sure it's anything worth following up on. I did make you an appointment for today at four o'clock."

"They may eat me alive with questions if I go in there today." Cora could just imagine all of the women descending on her wanting information about today's events.

"You're right," Amanda nodded. "Maybe I should cancel it."

"Hold off," Cora said. "Let's wait and see what information Wink decides to release today. If he announces the identity, then there won't be much more to tell."

§

"Wink," Officer Adam Reynolds said, walking around the piles of garbage spilled across the garage floor. "What do I do with these?" Officer Reynolds held up an evidence bag in each hand. Both contained cell phones.

"Just a second," Wink said into his cell phone and then placed it against his chest. "You got two phones out of there?"

"Yeah. This one belongs to the victim." Adam Reynolds held one bag forward.

"How do you know that?" Wink frowned.

"It was inside a leather pouch on his belt. The other was just loose."

"Dried blood on them?"

"Only on the unknown," Reynolds said. "The pouch protected this one."

"Good. We might need information off that phone. The other one can go to the lab."

"The batteries are dead. We'll need to charge them."

"We don't need to charge that one," Wink said pointing at the phone that did not belong to Owen Hollingsworth.

"Don't you want to see who owns it? It might be relevant."

"Okay, then. Fine. Set them both aside and we'll see if we can charge them." Wink motioned Adam Reynolds away with an angry glare and returned to his call. "Sorry, hon. People asking questions and then telling me how to answer."

"You have to eat, Wink," Mitzi said. "You can't work all night. Come by the house and I'll make you something."

"I'll try, but I can't promise. If we can sift through this and lock it up at a decent hour, I'll come over. I still have a lot to do."

"Okay, but I won't keep you."

"You know I'll want to stay too long, if I come over and there just isn't time for that." Mitzi's playful giggle made him blush. "We'll do something special once the Chief comes back. I'll make it up to you. I *can* promise that."

§

Cora's cell phone rang from her purse as she tried to juggle her dinner and her purse through the door. Dropping it all on the kitchen table, she dug out her phone. "Connie!"

"Cora, you're huffing and puffing again."

"You just caught me coming in the side door and I got all discombobulated trying to get my phone out and not drop my dinner."

"What a complicated life you lead," Conrad said chuckling. "What's for dinner tonight?"

"Well, Jo Anne made me a little pan of ravioli to take home and I just have to heat it up."

"I thought you told me you were only going to eat salad this week. Some new crazy diet idea."

"Yeah, well that didn't work out so well," Cora said. "It's cold and rainy here and I needed warm comfort food."

"I understand," Conrad said. "Would you like me to call back later? Let you have some dinner?"

"No, no. I needed to call you anyway. Amanda is starting to get answers on that ad in the paper and it seems that several people saw Joe Barney go down North Road on Friday night."

"Wink must have talked with him by now."

"No, I don't think so," Cora said. "I talked to him, but I didn't know all this then. He didn't tell me anything about going out of town that evening. He said he ran by Sesame Subs for a sandwich after work and took it home. Then he went to Sammy Lowe's party later that night."

"I'll tell him he needs to nail this down," Conrad said. "What time was it?"

"Hymie Morgan saw him about six o'clock heading away from town, but get this," Cora Mae said as she pulled open her oven door and slid the foil wrapped ravioli onto the middle of the rack. "He was in a blue truck. Hymie didn't think anything of it, because he didn't know what Joe usually drove."

"Barney was driving Owen's truck?"

"Sounds like it, but that's not all," Cora said, snapping the oven door closed and turning it on to warm. "Bryan Stotlar thinks he saw Joe Barney walking towards town just after sunset. Walking down the road, like maybe he ditched Owen's truck and—"

"Wait, wait," Conrad said. "Don't jump to conclusions. I'm hearing a lot of maybes in all this. Gather facts, not assumptions."

"I'm gathering whatever I can," Cora said with a grumble. "My feet hurt too much to jump to anything."

"I'll talk to Wink. He needs to have a formal interview with these poker buddies and tie them down on the evening events. There's another guy whose story is a bit off and it needs to be checked."

"Who?"

"Joshua Finley."

"Josh had a date," Cora said.

"Yes, but with whom? Did he tell you where he went?"

"No, but he didn't seem to be hiding it. I didn't ask any details."

"Well, his date said he didn't show up. He doesn't answer his phone either, because I tried to help the guys out and do some phone interviews from the hotel last night, but I didn't have much luck."

"Amanda got another tip today. Apparently, a couple of months ago when the construction project just started, Max Alvarez and Owen Hollingsworth got into a fight. The tipster said that Max hated Owen."

"He's on the interview list already."

"It surprised me because I see them both regularly and I don't detect any animosity between them."

"Maybe they fought and it's over now. Guys are like that." Conrad tossed Briscoe a treat and patted the bed for Briscoe to jump up.

"Maybe?" Cora huffed in mock indignation. "Why is it okay for you to say it?"

"It just is!" Conrad laughed. "I know. You're right. We'll check it out."

"Jo Biglioni said Owen has been in the Old Thyme Italian Restaurant and had dinner recently with someone she doesn't know. A man from out of town, I guess. She said she's seen him twice with the same guy. The last time was a couple of weeks ago."

Conrad scribbled that down in his notebook. Maybe Owen's wife would know about it. "Okay."

"And Owen was in Paxton two days before he disappeared. He was seen in the parking lot of the mall."

"Wednesday?"

"Wednesday evening," Cora said.

"Was that one of Amanda's tips?"

"No," Cora said. "It's a beauty shop tip."

"Oh, okay," Conrad said. "That's why you're late getting home tonight. You've jumped on the gossip bandwagon."

"Conrad Harris, how many years have you known me? You know I don't jump."

Conrad laughed.

"I have my own sources," Cora said adamantly. "I was gathering facts and getting my hair done. It's called multi-tasking."

"Okay, the mall on Wednesday. Who was he with?"

"Lillian said he was just walking to his truck and spoke to her. He was alone and didn't have anything in his hands. If he was shopping, he didn't buy anything."

"Okay, I'll see what the wife knows. You go eat dinner and I'll check with you tomorrow. I'm going to try and get home tomorrow if I can talk them into certifying Briscoe. He's done everything they've asked and told me what I need to know. I don't think we need another day here."

"I've got a couple of people to talk to tomorrow. Let me know if Alice gets back with you."

"I will. Good night."

"Night, Connie." Cora disconnected the call and pulled open the oven door to peek at dinner.

"Let me change clothes and then we'll eat."

Marmalade meowed in protest. She was already dressed for dinner.

§

"Good evening, Mrs. Hollingsworth. It's Chief Harris again. I hope I'm not calling too late."

"Of course not, Chief," Bonita Hollingsworth said. "Please, call me Bonita. What can I do for you?"

"I just had a few questions about your husband's union activity. I'm told he was a union member?"

"Oh, yes. Always has been, and he represents the union on the job site. If any of the guys have a problem, they come to Owen. He was very active when he was younger and trained a number of people, too. He enjoyed teaching."

"What kind of involvement has he had recently? Does he go to meetings or anything?"

"He does," Bonita said. "I called them on Monday, though, and they said they haven't seen him."

"Yes, we talked with them, but did Owen talk about these meetings with you at all? Was it a big group meeting or just him meeting with a representative?"

"He didn't really say, Chief. I assumed it was a big group. They were usually weeknights and they were dinner meetings because he told me I didn't need to cook. He was always home shortly after eight or so. They weren't late."

"Would the other guys that he worked with go to these meetings, too? Joe Barney, for instance. Would he have been there? We can always check with him."

"They are all members, but Owen never said anything about who attended. Was there a meeting on Friday night? Are you thinking he went there instead of to the derby?"

"No," Conrad said. "Not Friday, but there have been some recently. I think there was one last Wednesday night. Do you remember if he went to that one?"

"No, actually I don't," Bonita said. "Wait, no. He was working on one of those derby cars that night. He was late for dinner, I remember."

"One last question," Conrad said. "Do you know Max Alvarez?"

"Not personally, Chief, but Owen has mentioned him. They are working together on the community building."

"Yes. Did they get along okay? Did Owen say anything about having any disagreements with any of his coworkers?"

"Oh, no," Bonita said. "Not his coworkers, but he did tell me once that his supervisor was upset with him. I asked him about it, but he just laughed it off like it was nothing."

"I know this is difficult, and I'm sorry to keep asking questions of you, Mrs. Hollingsworth. We do appreciate all your help, though."

"You didn't know Owen, Chief. He was the easiest guy in the world to get along with. Everyone always liked him," Bonita said with a crack in her voice. "I can't believe this happened because someone disliked him. It had to have been a horrible accident."

"Thank you again, and I'll stop by and see you once I'm back in town."

"Thank you, Chief. Good night."

Conrad tapped his phone to disconnect and glanced at Briscoe. "I wish that made sense, but his truck didn't drive itself north of town."

Briscoe opened his eyes slightly and then fell back asleep.

CHAPTER 20

"Good morning, Miss Morgan." Harvey Salzman poked his head around the door frame to Amanda's outer office.

"Good morning, Mr. Salzman! How are you?"

"Oh, pretty good. It's not too cold yet and the rain's stopped, so I got my walk in this morning. You know, once it gets too chilly, I don't get out so much."

"Yes, and it's headed that way." Amanda smiled as Harvey Salzman walked into the office. "What can I do for you today?"

"I was just peeking in to see if the mayor might be free. You know I hate to bother her, but I hate not to bother her and find out later that I knew something she didn't. Maybe she needs to know. I just never know. Is she in?"

"Morning, Saucy," Cora called out as she walked toward her office door at the sound of his voice. "I thought I heard you out here talking in circles. What are you up to today?"

"Well, Mayor, I don't want you to get to thinkin' that I only carry bad news, but I was just out taking my morning walk and there's some activity down at your construction site again."

"Oh, no. Is someone hurt?"

"No ambulance this time," Saucy said holding up his hands. "But there is a police car parked on the front curb and a little group gathered up. It looked like something was up to me, so I thought I'd stop in and let you know. With Chief Harris out, I thought you might not have heard."

"I'm hoping the Chief gets to come back today. I just don't know what to think about all this commotion down at the construction site."

"It's a sad thing," Saucy said shaking his head. "A real shame about Hollingsworth."

"Makes me wonder if this project may have not been one of my better ideas." Cora Mae grimaced.

"Don't say that," Saucy said. "It's going to be a great thing for this town. It looks like it's going to be real fancy down there and we can have all kinds of special events in town."

"I agree," Amanda added. "It's going to be beautiful. Everyone's going to love it."

"I just need it to finish without any more problems. We are getting close to having the outside done and then the finishing work inside can get started."

"Will it be done by Christmas?" Saucy said.

"Oh, yes. I was planning to have it open in October. These problems have caused some delays, of course, but I'm sure we'll be able to hold holiday events there this year."

"Fingers crossed!" Saucy waved as he turned toward the door. "Have a good day, ladies."

"You, too, Saucy. Take care." Cora hesitated in a moment of indecision. "I guess I'll try to call the PD and see what's happening down there. I wasn't planning to stop by the construction site today. I have other work to do."

"Would you like me to call for you?" Amanda reached for the phone.

"Yes, that would helpful," Cora said as she turned to go back to her office. "Georgia should be on dispatch today. I'll catch up with Wink later. Thank you."

§

"Good morning, Coroner," Wink said. "I'm sorry for the delay but I just got your message."

"Good morning, Wink," Alice said as papers rustled on her desk. "Let me find my report. Have you heard from Conrad?"

"Yes, ma'am. He's hoping he'll be able to return this evening. If he gets that training certificate, he'll hit the road."

"What do you think of his dog? I haven't seen him yet."

"Oh, he's a fine mutt," Wink said with a chuckle. "I'm not sure what his breed really is, but he's got to be part human."

"It was nice to hear he came from your shelter. I don't think everyone realizes that shelters are full of exceptional animals that make very special pets."

"And coworkers," Wink laughed. "I think he outranks me already."

Alice laughed. "Don't feel bad. I have a houseful, and they all think I work for them."

Wink heard a file cabinet drawer slam shut as he waited for the coroner's report. "Did the spouse get in touch with you?"

"She did. My deputy, Alan York, talked to her about those arrangements. We've finished the preliminary post-mortem exam and the cause of death is a blow to the head, but I'm sure you expected that."

"Yeah," Wink said with a nervous swallow.

"The only noteworthy issue is lividity. The head blow was to the back of the head, and you would expect him to die prone if someone or something struck him from behind. That makes you fall forward, but the lividity shows him supine, on his back."

"So, he didn't die in the dumpster," Wink said. "He was moved there."

"With the amount of blood present, I'd say he probably bled out in the dumpster."

"Oh," Wink shuddered. He didn't like this part of the job.

"On his back," Alice added. "You'll tell the Chief?"

"Yeah, sure."

"I'll email a report over."

"Okay. Thank you," Wink said, hanging up Conrad's office phone and pulling out his cell to text Conrad a message. The sooner he could relay the coroner's message, the sooner he could quit thinking about it.

§

"Mandy," Cora called out from her desk. "Did you ever reach Georgia to find out what was going on down at the community center?"

Amanda leaned in Cora's doorway. "I did. She said they were just there to file a theft report. They've got some tools missing."

"Again!" Cora leaned back in her chair. "You'd think they'd do something to nip this problem in the bud. It keeps happening. Why don't they take measures to check on their equipment before they leave at night? I don't understand it."

"What do they do with their tools at the end of the day?"

"Apparently some of the guys use their personal tools for every day and they take those home, but the big stuff is supposed to be signed out for use during the day. When it's returned, they are supposed to lock it up for the night."

"So, they aren't returning it?" Amanda asked with a scrunched-up face. "But the sign out sheet would show who took it."

"You'd think so, wouldn't you?" Cora threw up her hands in the air. "Turns out, the person on the sheet just denies ever checking the tool out and they don't know who has anything around there. It's crazy."

"A seriously flawed system." Amanda shook her head in amazement.

"Indeed. It's almost like they want the thefts to continue," Cora said with a frown. "Hmm, why would... Mandy, who is the union down there? Do we know what chapter or who the local contact is for the union that Owen would have been under?"

"Maybe it's in our building contract. I can look." Amanda pulled open a filing cabinet drawer behind Cora's office door and squatted down.

"I don't know if Wink talked to them about Owen or about the thefts, but someone needs to. I'll be glad when the Chief gets back. I just don't feel like I know what's going on down there."

"It looks like there are different unions for different kinds of workers. It's not just one group," Amanda said, holding open a file. "There's a whole list."

"I need to ask Alan Avery," Cora said. "I know he's talked to Owen's union, and he probably has all the contact information."

"Oh, I got another tip from the newspaper this morning, but it may be nothing. The email said there were two trucks parked at the construction site after hours Friday night. One was blue and the other white, but the blue one was gone by seven o'clock."

"Did you forward that to the PD?"

"I did. The email wasn't signed, but I know the email address."

Cora smiled. "Who was it?"

"The email address belongs to Julie Cason."

"The veterinarian?" Dr. Cason specialized in small animals, while Amanda's father, Hymie Morgan, was primarily the local farm vet.

"Yeah, the email was sent from her office account, but it wasn't signed. It could be someone who works for her."

"True, but hopefully someone will make some inquiries. It sounds like it could have been Owen's truck, but it may just have been when Owen and Alan Avery stayed late to talk that night. I don't know what Alan drives."

"Do all the guys that are working down there drive trucks?"

"Almost all of them, and there are a lot of white trucks on my list, if I remember." Cora opened her desk drawer and pulled out her index cards from her first set of interviews down at the construction site. "Yes, Joe Barney, Josh Finley, Cy McDaniels, and

Cheryl Pittman all had white trucks. Some of the guys drive different vehicles from day to day, so I don't have that listed for everyone. That's another thing that Alan Avery might know, though."

"Sometimes people just park and walk somewhere else after hours. It could have been completely unrelated."

"That's true," Cora sighed and leaned back in her chair. "Without a license number... Maybe I need to go back down there. I was going to skip my visit today, but there are just too many unanswered questions. I think I'll stop by after lunch and see if I can catch Alan free."

"And check out the white trucks in the parking lot?" Amanda laughed.

"And that," Cora winked.

§

"What's up with the phones, Tabor?" Wink walked out to the dispatch area after getting coffee in the break room. He had been tempted to use the Chief's coffeepot in his office but was afraid the Chief would detect it. He had been offered the office, not the coffeepot, and the Chief was very protective.

"Well, this one," Officer Eugene Tabor said as he pointed to the phone on his right, "It belonged to the deceased."

"Owen Hollingsworth," Wink said, walking up to look over Eugene's shoulder.

"It required a password, but I called his wife and she gave me the code. I'm still going through it."

"Anything on the other phone?"

"Oh, yeah. This one belongs to Joshua Finley and there's plenty going on there." Tabor laughed as he handed the phone to Wink. "It's a reality show in the making."

"A reality show?" Wink frowned and took the phone from Tabor.

"It's like a soap opera."

"Ah, he's a busy guy with the ladies. I already had one of them chew me out because Finley stood her up Friday night."

"Must be Melody." Tabor smirked. "I think he went out with Sandy Teague instead. The guy is tempting fate. This is a small town, and they're all going to run into each other at some point in time."

"Sounds like you speak from experience," Wink chuckled.

"Not me, boss. I'm not crazy."

"I guess we need to talk with Sandy Teague and confirm times. He was late getting to the poker party, too. We need to find out how the phone ended up in the dumpster."

"If I had women all yelling at me in texts like he did, I'd throw my own phone away!" Tabor turned in his chair to prop his feet up in the chair beside him. "This other phone, Owen's phone, it has some weird messages on it. They aren't from Friday night, but he was setting meetings up with a couple of people, and it's not clear what's going on. Did he have some side job or something?"

"Not that I know of," Wink said. "He was pretty deep in with the demolition derby cars, and I know he worked in the pit crews there. Maybe they're car guys."

"Maybe," Tabor said, leaning back in his chair and holding the phone up to scroll through the list. "He's not good about setting up his contacts, so most of them just have first names. I can't tell who they are."

"I'll call over and see if we can get phone records on him, but that could take some time. For now, just make some notes on the last few weeks of calls or texts and we'll work on those."

"Wink," Georgia called out from the dispatch booth as Wink started down the hallway. "We got another theft report from the construction site this morning. I put a copy on the Chief's desk."

"Okay. Thanks, Georgie. I think I'm going to run down to the site and see if I can talk to Josh Finley about his phone. I can't call him, so I guess I need to try and catch him before he leaves work today."

CHAPTER 21

"Come in," Alan Avery yelled out as Cora popped the trailer door open.

"Hi, Alan."

"Oh, Mrs. B! I thought you were one of the guys. This isn't your regular time. Busy day?"

"Oh, well I wasn't planning to come by today, but something has come up and I know this is an imposition, but do you suppose I could just talk with Joe Barney for a minute?"

"That shouldn't be a problem. He's up on the second floor, hanging a door on one of the offices. Do you want me to go and get him for you?"

"Oh, no. That won't be necessary. I'll go up and try to catch him at a free moment. Can I ask you a few questions first, Alan?"

"Sure."

"I assume you are familiar with all the vehicles that the guys drive to work. I'm missing some from my list and I thought maybe you would know."

"Some of them change out once in a while, but I think I know most of them. You know Owen drove an old blue truck," Alan said.

"Yes, and I have several notes here about white trucks. Are there a lot of them or did I put that down wrong?"

Alan laughed. "No, you're right. There are a lot of them. Josh Finley, Joe Barney and Cy McDaniels all drive a white pickup. Different models, but they're all white. Once in a while, Ken Hardy will drive his white truck, but most days he's in a little blue sedan. He drives from Paxton every day and he says it gets better gas mileage."

"I have Cheryl Pittman as having a white truck, too."

"Yep," Alan said. "I forgot about her. She's not here every day, but she does drive a white pickup, too."

"How does anyone know which one is theirs at the end of the day?" Cora giggled. "Do you have one too, Alan?"

"I do, as a matter of fact." Alan laughed as he leaned back in his chair. "I guess I just add to the confusion."

"The little red car out there," Cora said, pointing to the front of the building. "That belongs to Max Alvarez, right?"

"Yeah."

"I had another question that you can probably explain for me. I don't know how the union works here. The contract shows a whole list of different ones. Are the guys all in different unions?"

"They're separated by the type of trade they do," Alan said, leaning forward in his chair. "The plumbers have their own trade union, as do the electricians, et cetera. Owen was in the carpenters' union. The construction company has to keep all that straight because their contracts are a little different. It is confusing."

"But you had dealings with Owen's union, didn't you?"

"Yes, from time to time. We had some inquiries about work issues and his union came to represent him. That's what they do. We also contact them when we have to change something or advise them of something that happened. When Donny McBride was hurt, we let his union rep know. Stuff like that."

"So," Cora said. "You know all these reps?"

"Not all of them, but I've met several. Owen's rep was Parnell Dooley. He's worked for the carpenters' union for years, so I've had different occasions to talk with him."

"Do they ever show up on the work site or look around?"

"Not during the workday. There have been some rare occasions when they've come inside a property to look at something, but that's usually because they've received a complaint about work conditions or something like that. That hasn't happened on this job at all."

"I've learned so much during this project," Cora said, smiling. "I never really knew how all of this worked before. It's very interesting."

"It's definitely its own little world."

"One more thing. Cheryl Pittman. She's a welder, right?"

"Yeah, so we only need her once in a while."

"Was she here last Friday?"

"No, not on Friday," Alan said. "She had been here earlier in that week and was due the following

Monday. The last job Owen did was to put up supports for her to come in on Monday."

"I keep missing her. I've met her, but I've not talked to her since Owen's accident."

"Is that what it is?" Alan said. "Was it an accident? No one has told us anything."

"That's what I'm calling it for now." Cora stood up and smiled. "I'll see if I can go find Joe before he leaves, and thanks for the information."

"Anytime, Mrs. B."

Cora grabbed her pink hard hat and weaved through the workers walking up and down the stairs. The drywall was all finished in the front offices and Joe Barney was in the doorway. Down the hallway, she saw Wink off to the side talking with Josh Finley, but his back was toward her.

"Hey, Joe. How are you today?"

"Hi, Mayor. I'm good. Are you here to check out the office? They'll probably start painting tomorrow."

"Wonderful. It is all coming along nicely." Cora looked around the room and saw Cy McDaniels working on one of the windows. "When you get done here, do you think I could have a word with you, Joe?"

"Sure, Mayor. I'll be done here in just a minute."

"I'll just look around a little, and I'll come back. You take your time. I don't want to interrupt." Cora walked to the next office off the hallway and saw Cody Beck working with Ken Hardy to finish the drywall in that office. Everything was covered in a white powder and Cora could feel a grittiness in the back of her throat as she cupped her hand over her mouth to wave. At the end of the hallway, a long floor-length window had been removed to allow access for a crane to deliver materials to the second floor. The opening continued to be used for trash removal, and Cora walked cautiously near the opening to look down at the area marked off with crime scene tape.

"What can I do for you, Mayor?" Cora gasped in shock and spun around on her heel. Joe Barney was inches away, grinning in delight at startling her. Adrenaline was forcing Cora's heartbeat to pound in her ears and she felt lightheaded from just imagining a fall from that opening.

"Oh, Joe. I didn't see you. I just have a quick question."

"Sure thing."

"I don't know if you read The Spicetown Star, but I put an ad in the paper to help find Owen or find people who had seen him."

"Yeah, I saw the ad in the paper."

"Well, we're still getting information from that," Cora said. "It has become a bit of an unofficial tip line, if you will."

"Really?" Joe looked down at his legs and brushed off his pant legs. "That's good, I guess."

"Yes, the folks in town here are very helpful. I know we talked earlier, but my notes are a little sketchy. Can you tell me again how it was the last night Owen worked, that Friday night?"

"The two of us worked on the front supports that day. He quit early to go talk to Alan. I think Alan had set up the meeting, but that's the last I saw of him."

"What time did you leave work that Friday?"

"Around five o'clock, I think. We punch out, so you can check the timecards."

"I meant actually leave the premises," Cora said. "I know you guys quit work sometimes and hang around to chat or clean up. There was a party planned that night. I thought maybe you hung around to talk."

"Not that I remember."

"Did you drive your white truck that Friday?"

"Yeah."

"You're sure?" Cora cocked her head to the side.

"I'm sure. It's the only truck I've got. Why do you ask?"

"Did you come back to the job site after five o'clock? Maybe you forgot something?" Cora tensed as Joe stepped forward, but he quickly stepped back and looked at the floor.

"No, I didn't come back here." Joe Barney glanced down the hallway and saw Wink standing near the doorway to the front office.

"We have a report from someone who saw you driving Owen's truck Friday night."

"What? They're wrong! That wasn't me. I told you what I did. I got a sandwich and went home to clean up."

"Yes, you told me that, but you were late to the party. Did you come back here before you went to the party?"

"No. I was home. I didn't feel like going right off. I was just watching some TV and relaxing. Nothing special."

"We have another report of a meeting here later, after hours—"

"That wasn't me!" Joe shouted as he kicked a wood piece against the wall, and Cora's eyes darted to connect with Wink's. He had finished his talk with Joshua Finley and was hovering near the office door to keep an eye on Cora.

"Joe, I'm not accusing. I'm just asking. Maybe you forgot a quick trip back here to pick up something, or a small errand you ran that evening that would explain the sightings. Did you see anybody before you went to the party?" Cora held her hands out defensively when she saw anger in Joe's eyes.

"I'm sorry, Mayor. This has just been a really stressful time. Owen has been my buddy for a long time and you never expect something like this to happen to anybody you know. I didn't mean to yell."

"No, I'm sorry to keep bringing up these things, but we just want to find the answers."

"I know."

"So," Cora said, shifting her stance, so the opening wasn't directly behind her. "You weren't walking down North Road that Friday night?"

"No," Joe said shaking his head. "Wait. Someone said I was here and somebody else said I was walking down the road?"

"Yes," Cora shrugged. "But at different times that evening."

"I did just what I told you. None of that was me."

"Your truck was home all evening until you went over to Sammy's party?"

"Yeah, like I said, it's the only one I've got."

"How is Owen's wife doing? Have you talked with her in the last few days?" Cora hoped to ease the tension.

"No. I keep thinking I need to, but I'm just not ready to talk yet. You know?" Joe looked up and met Cora's eyes deliberately as the muscles in his face were fighting off a scowl.

"I know. I won't keep you any longer. I know you have work to do. Thank you for taking a minute."

"Sure, Mayor." Joe walked away with his eyes down and turned sideways to pass Wink with a nod.

Wink strolled over to where Cora remained standing. "Mayor? Everything okay?"

"Yes, Wink. Come closer," Cora said, motioning him over with a wave. "Look down there." Cora pointed out the opening. "You see where the dumpster was?"

"Yeah."

"You know how Alice said he hit the back of his head, but landed on his back, which was odd?"

"Yeah."

"I think he fell from this opening and hit his head on the edge of the dumpster when he fell in. You remember the inside of the dumpster was..." Cora waved her hands and scrunched up her face.

"Brain matter," Wink forced the words out with a groan.

Cora shuddered and grabbed Wink's arm as she lowered her voice. "I think he was pushed."

CHAPTER 22

"Hop in, Briscoe." Conrad pointed to the open car door. "We're headed home, boy." Conrad slammed the car door and got into the driver's seat. He had left voice mail messages for Wink and Cora to let them know he was heading back to Spicetown but hadn't talked with either of them.

"You know, I'm a little bit worried," Conrad said, glancing at Briscoe. "When I can't reach Cora or Wink in the middle of the day, that makes me think they're up to something."

Conrad paused as if Briscoe was telepathically answering him.

"I know. I know, but Cora Mae can get herself into a pickle sometimes and I don't think Wink realizes the lengths she will go to find something out. He might disregard a suggestion she makes, and she'll take out on her own. You have to incorporate her into your investigation, or you waste time following her around to keep an eye out. It's not productive."

Conrad stroked his hand down Briscoe's back and they both relaxed as the city expressway turned into a simple divided highway pointed toward Ohio.

"We should make it home shortly after dark."

Conrad tapped his console to call the office phone number and Sam Crawford, the evening dispatcher, answered. "Hey, Chief."

"Sammy. I know it's shift change, but is Tabor still around the office?"

"No, Chief. He's already gone for the day."

"Do you know where Wink is right now?"

"Georgia told me before she left that he went down to the construction site. He hasn't reported in since I've been on duty."

"Hmm, okay. Well, I'm on my way back, but if Wink shows up, can you ask him to stick around or give me a call? I'd like to talk to him tonight."

"Sure thing, Chief. See you soon."

Conrad glanced at the time and knew there was no one at the construction site this late in the day. Cora Mae was probably trying to make her way home and arrange dinner. He didn't want to call in the middle of that and have her huffing and puffing again to answer.

Wink was not reporting into the office as he should be. Wink was accustomed to being on night patrol where there's always a radio nearby. He was forgetting that dispatch could not track him so easily as Acting Chief. One week had not been enough time for Wink to learn how important accountability is when you're Police Chief. Every minute of your time belongs to your town.

Conrad tapped his console to call Cora Mae again. The driving time was dragging, and he was anxious to know what was going on. When the call went to voice mail, he stabbed the disconnect button on the screen.

"Where is everybody?" Briscoe lifted one eyebrow and Conrad concurred. "I hate to stir up the town, but you're right. Someone needs to find out."

Conrad hit the dispatch number on his console. "Sammy?"

"Yeah, Chief?"

"Send a car over to the construction site and see if Wink is still over there. It's after hours for the workers. Make sure everything looks right over there."

"I tried to get him on radio, but he's not answering. I can send Jennings over."

"Did he drive down to the site?" Conrad squirmed in his seat and increased his cruising speed slightly.

"No, Chief. His patrol car is in the lot. He must have walked down."

"He should have come back by now."

"Hang on, Chief."

Conrad could hear the crackle of the radio and Sammy responding.

"Chief, Jennings is going down there to look around."

"Okay. Let me know." Conrad disconnected the call with a huff.

"Where is everybody?" Conrad smacked his hand on the steering wheel. Briscoe's eyebrow raised again, and Conrad laughed at himself. "I know. I already asked you that, and you're right. I'm getting a little uptight about it. I'll try to be patient." Conrad exhaled through pursed lips and tapped his console again to see his navigation screen. The Ohio state line was nearing as his anxiety increased.

"You're probably dreaming about dinner, aren't you?" Conrad scratched Briscoe's ear. "I'm a little hungry myself. We'll take care of that as soon as we get back to Spicetown."

"Hey, Sammy," Conrad said after stabbing the telephone icon that was flashing on his console.

"Chief, Wink isn't at the factory. Jennings checked it all out and there's nobody down there."

"If he's on foot, he can't be far. Maybe he stopped to get something to eat." Conrad tried to crawl inside Wink's head and think what he might do as he walked from the construction site to the police department. Sammy was answering a radio call in the background.

"Chief, Hudson said there are lights on in City Hall. Anything going on up there that you know about?"

"No, but I tried to call the mayor's cell phone earlier and she didn't answer. Tell him to go check it out."

"Okay. I'll let you know." Sammy disconnected the phone and Conrad increased his speed when he saw he was nearing the bridge that would take him over the Ohio River and home to Spicetown.

"I should probably stop by the sub shop and get something to eat. You know there's nothing at the house," Conrad said, glancing over at Briscoe who had straightened up in his seat to peer out the windshield when the car turned to go over the bridge.

"I don't understand why I haven't heard back from Cora. That's not like her. She doesn't run around town at night and it's late enough that she should be relaxing at home. Maybe there's something wrong with her phone."

Briscoe looked left and then right as they entered a small town on the Ohio River border. "Or maybe there's just something wrong. She wouldn't work up at City Hall this late at night, would she? Why hasn't Sammy called?"

Meandering through the small town was stressful as Conrad had to minimize his speed. As he finally broke free of the town, his console told him the PD was calling back.

"Yeah, Sammy."

"His key doesn't work, Chief. He's got to run back to the office and get another. Nobody answered the front doors when he rattled them."

"Why doesn't his key work?"

"He said he's never tried it before. He didn't know, but it doesn't turn." Conrad had sent Asher to the hardware store to have duplicates made when Jennings was hired, and they should have tested them all.

"Is Co—, is the mayor's car there?"

"Around back. That's the only car there. I tried calling the City Hall number but no answer. I didn't really expect anybody to pick up at this hour, but I thought I'd give it a try."

"Thanks, Sam. I'm real close to town now, so unless I hear from you, I'll head straight to City Hall."

"Okay, Chief. I'll let Jennings know."

Conrad disconnected and punched the speed dial number for Wink's cell phone. "He needs to answer," Conrad said as Briscoe stared back at him.

When the voice mail message began to play, Conrad tried to calm himself with a deep breath before speaking.

"I don't know where you are, but the bigger problem is that NOBODY knows where you are," Conrad shouted. "This can't keep happening. If you get this message before I find you, it would behoove you to call me back swiftly."

Conrad slapped the disconnect button and then had to punch it twice to get it to turn off. He squeezed the steering wheel to release the anger that slamming a phone receiver would relieve.

"It's such a simple thing," Conrad shouted but softened when Briscoe crinkled his eyebrows in concern. "I'm okay. I'd just like to strangle someone. That's all." Briscoe stayed alert and watchful. "I hope we find Wink soon, because he is my first choice."

Briscoe turned to look out the side window as if he recognized Spicetown.

"I see Jennings down here. You may get your first chance to search a building." Conrad rubbed the scruff of Briscoe's neck as Briscoe whined in anticipation of release.

Conrad pulled up next to Jennings's patrol car and pushed open his car door. Climbing out stiffly from the driver's side seat, he pushed off against the door to straighten his back and motioned to Briscoe that he could get out, too.

"Hey, Chief." Officer Jennings stood on the front steps of City Hall. His patrol car was running, and the headlights were shining on the front doors.

"No luck?" Conrad walked up the steps with Briscoe on his heels.

"I still can't get in. I went back to the station and got another set of keys, but I can't get these to turn either."

"Let me try. We may have to go around the back. Sometimes if you shake it..." Conrad wiggled the key and pulled the door handle towards his body to get the deadbolt to slide smoothly. "It doesn't line up quite right."

The bolt snapped open and Conrad yanked the front doors apart to walk into the dark lobby. The lights shining through the window from the street were only in Cora Mae's office. Pausing in the dark, he listened first and held up his hand for Jennings to follow quietly. The door to Amanda's outer office was on the side of the lobby. It was shut, but the light shown underneath the door. Cora's office was only accessible by walking through Amanda's office.

Standing close to the door, Conrad listened to the voices before reaching for the doorknob. He could hear Cora Mae talking, but was waiting to see if there was another person in the room.

§

"I know we have a difference of opinion on this," Cora Mae said. "But I think he had time. Take a look at this." Cora tapped a drawing she had made of the construction site on one side of town and North Road, where Owen's car was found.

"This is Sammy Lowe's house. He's the young man who drives the backhoe. You may not have met him yet, but he had the party Friday night at his house." Cora took a red marker and circled the house. "This is Joe Barney's house."

Wink nodded.

"Now, I specifically asked him about this, and he had plenty of chances to tell me he saw his ex-wife Friday night."

"Maybe she's lying," Wink said as he leaned forward against Cora's conference table and propped his elbow on the table to rest his chin in his palm. "He owed her money. They're divorced. Domestics aren't trustworthy."

"What does she have to gain? He can't pay child support if he's in jail."

"That's logic. Domestics aren't logical. They're all about revenge."

"Wink Hobson, you are a stubborn, acrimonious man! If the situation were reversed and it was Joe talking about her, would you feel the same way?"

"If it's true, why didn't she contact police about this or send in an email when you put your ad in the paper?"

"Nobody asked for information about Joe Barney's whereabouts," Cora said throwing her hands in the air. "She had no way to know this was connected. This is your tip, not mine."

"Nothing coming out of the beauty shop is a tip. It's just a hen party and they're telling tales." Wink threw back his shoulders and leaned against the chair. "I just mentioned it because—"

"That's where I heard the tip about you finding the truck out on North Road. The hens at the beauty shop have been surprisingly accurate in regards to this case because they've had an excellent source of information."

"I know," Wink said holding up his hands to calm their discussion. "I made a mistake—"

"You made more than one." Conrad stood in Cora Mae's doorway with his hands on his hips and a scowl on his face. "You might just hear about them if you turn on your phone because your voice mail is full of them."

Wink jerked back in his chair in alarm and Cora threw her hands up in the air.

"Oh, Connie. I'm so glad you're back. I guess Briscoe is all certified now?"

At the sound of his name, Briscoe whined and looked to Conrad for consent before greeting Cora.

Conrad nodded and Cora held out her hands to stroke Briscoe's head. "Were you a good boy?" Cora cooed.

"No one has been able to reach either one of you all evening." Conrad walked into the room and turned to Wink. "Did you forget that you are Acting Chief? That you told your staff you were going to the construction site three hours ago and they never heard from you again? Do you know how to operate a cell phone?" Conrad's voice boomed in the deserted building.

"Sorry. Sorry, Chief," Wink said as he scrambled his long legs up under him to stand. "The phone hasn't..." Wink pulled his cell phone from his belt and glanced at the display. "I didn't know the ringer was off. I was interviewing and turned it—"

"So, no. You failed to operate your cell phone properly." Conrad walked around behind Wink and shook his head.

"I guess I did. I finished my interview and went to talk to the mayor about hers. We were there at the same time and got to talking—"

"It's a good thing nothing big happened while you two were chatting. Nobody had a wreck, needed emergency response, or fell off a building. Isn't it? Isn't it lucky that everything went okay?" Conrad continued to pace as his volume intensified.

"Yes, Chief," Wink said, spinning around to face Conrad. "Lucky."

Cora kept her eyes on Briscoe and spoke softly. "You're right, Chief. We should have touched base. I think my phone ringer was probably turned off, too, and we were focused on the information we'd gathered today. We were consolidating our theories."

Conrad ignored Cora's excuse.

"I think you're off duty for the day, Officer Hobson. You can write me a report tomorrow on your events and return to evening shift."

"Yes, sir," Wink said quietly as he pushed in his chair to the conference table.

"Officer Jennings," Conrad said to Adam Jennings who remained in the mayor's doorway. "I'd like you to stay around until the mayor safely locks up and makes it to her car."

"Yes, sir," Jennings said with a nod as he moved sideways to let Wink leave the room.

"Chief, we do have a lot of information we need to share with you," Cora said timidly.

"I look forward to hearing about it tomorrow," Conrad said, looking only at Briscoe. "Come on, boy."

Officer Adam Jennings jumped out of the doorway again to let Conrad and Briscoe exit as Cora Mae said, "Goodnight."

CHAPTER 23

Conrad sat at his desk the next morning with his reading glasses on his nose and a coffee cup in his hand as he perused the interviews in the Owen Hollingsworth case file. His door was shut, which was rare, but he was still decompressing from the disappointment of the previous evening and didn't want to engage with his staff yet. Briscoe was napping on his fleece-covered memory foam bed by the window.

After his second cup of coffee, he removed his glasses and reached for the phone.

"Good morning. I'm Chief Harris with the Spicetown Police Department. Is this Cheryl Pittman?" Conrad could hear banging in the background and wind blowing against the phone receiver.

"This is Cheryl. Hi, Chief. I'm sorry I missed your call yesterday, but I was probably welding, and I don't hear anything during that."

"That's quite all right. Do you have a moment to talk now? Is it a good time?"

"Yes, I can talk. I'm just waiting at a job site right now. They aren't ready for me yet. Let me get inside my truck so I can hear you better."

"Okay." Conrad waited until the background noise diminished.

"What can I do for you?"

"Well, I was just wanting to touch base with you in regard to Owen Hollingsworth. He was the man found at the Spicetown Community Center job."

"Yeah, I knew Owen."

"Well, it doesn't look like you were on the job site on his last day there, but I thought you might be able to add something about his work or his relationships with his coworkers. How do you know Mr. Hollingsworth?"

"Ah, I've known him for years. He's been at a lot of jobs I've done. He's a nice guy. I'm not sure what would help you."

"Did you have occasion to talk with him on this job?"

"Sure. I mean we said hello, how are you, stuff like that."

"Anything odd or different about this time or this job?" Conrad said, searching for an example. "Did he act like his usual self?"

"Yeah, he's always friendly. I did see him arguing with his buddy, Joe, the last time I was there, though. Maybe they bicker all the time and I don't know it, but I'd not seen that before."

"Joe Barney?"

"Yeah, they work together all the time and I thought they were close friends. Two peas in a pod, you know. Usually, they are cutting up and joking around, but that day they were arguing in the parking lot when I was walking up to the building that morning."

"What day was this?"

"I was there the week before, on a Wednesday, just for the morning. I had some prep work to do and was walking around the side of the building to go to the office."

"Did they know you could hear them? Or could anyone else hear them?"

"No, they were out in the parking lot away from the other guys and I was walking through where the trucks were parked. I don't think they saw me."

"What did you hear?"

"They were shouting at each other," Cheryl said. "They were talking about the union and Joe was blaming Owen for something. He kept saying it was all Owen's fault and whatever it was made Joe mad. He tried to shut him down and told him he was crazy, that it wasn't true, but Joe was poking Owen's shoulder and Owen just kept backing up, trying to end the conversation. I kept moving and so I didn't hear the end of it."

"Do you have any idea what they were talking about?"

"No. I mean, when they mentioned the union, I thought Joe was accusing Owen of getting him in trouble with the union somehow. Maybe Owen told them something about Joe's work? I'm just guessing. It seemed work related, though."

"Do you know anything about the quality of their work? Either one of them?"

"Not really. I've never heard anything negative about them, and I know Owen is a union mentor, so I'd assume he does quality work."

"What time was this? First thing in the morning?" Conrad looked at his calendar. He had been in town that day.

"No, everybody else was already working. I'd say close to ten o'clock because I'd been at another site earlier that day."

"Did you talk to the supervisor or project manager about what you heard?"

"No, I just clocked in and let them know I was on site."

"Have you told anyone else about this?"

"No," Cheryl said.

"Have you talked to Joe Barney since then?"

"No, but I've seen him since. We don't really talk. I might wave or say hello, but that's about it."

"Okay. I appreciate your time and let me know if you think of anything else."

"Sure, Chief."

Conrad hung up the phone and looked at the scribbled notes he had taken when he tried to get the words down that Cheryl remembered hearing. Maybe Owen told the union something. Conrad read Wink's report on his conversation with Parnell Dooley again. That call had been right after the reported disappearance and didn't fully address the issues they now had before them.

Conrad wanted to get out of the office, and it looked like Parnell Dooley needed a visit.

§

"I passed the Chief on my way to work today," Amanda said as she crouched down to reach the bottom file cabinet drawer. "I bet you're glad to have him back in town."

"He got back in last night," Cora said. "I was still at the office talking with Wink when he arrived."

"I must have just missed you when I left yesterday, but I knew you had to come back to the office for your car. Was everything okay down at the work site?"

"Things are moving along nicely. They may be able to start painting today in one of the rooms. The glass entry way is going to be put up this week if the weather cooperates. After that, all the work needed is inside."

"Here is the list of recommendations I've received on the naming of the community center." Amanda held the list out to Cora. "Do you want the list copied for the City Council? I can add it to their meeting packets."

"No, I don't think I want to do that yet. I'd like to wait and see if we get anymore suggestions. I haven't seen anything on the list that catches my eye particularly. Have you?"

"I liked the idea of calling it Spicer Hall, but that really sounds more like a college campus building than a city community center."

"I'm waiting for something to grab me," Cora said, waving a fist in the air. "I've been calling it the community center so long; I may have a hard time with any other name."

"We got one complaint recently from an anonymous contributor. They heard about Briscoe and thought the town should have been involved in naming him."

"I don't think Briscoe needs to be a spice. He's Conrad's pet first and a city employee second. A dog's name has to fit their personality."

Amanda nodded as she pushed the file drawer shut. "I'm surprised the Chief hasn't stopped in."

"He has a lot of catching up to do."

"I saw you had new drawings on the table," Amanda said, pointing.

"Yes, I was going to ask you about that." Cora got up from her desk and walked over the conference table. "Did your mom say anything to you about Teresa Barney being in her shop?"

"She mentioned that Teresa told her that Joe was close friends with Owen. I think she said Joe was worried when Owen disappeared. Nothing else that I recall. Why?"

"Well, Wink had heard that Teresa was talking about seeing Joe walking on North Road that Friday night, just like Bryan said. I thought maybe she told your mom about it. I know it came from the beauty shop."

"She might have. I can ask her. I know Teresa is a customer down there."

"That's okay. I'll try to give Teresa a call and clarify it. I want to make sure it's true before I tell Conrad. He's always yelling about getting facts and not gossip. I don't want to tell him something wrong."

"Wink probably heard it from Mitzi," Amanda said.

"Are they still courting?"

"I think it's on hold." Amanda chuckled. "Mitzi got mad because Wink was always canceling their dates because he had to work. I guess she felt neglected and Mitzi finally told him she didn't want to talk to him again until the Chief came back."

"Have you and Mitzi become friends?"

"No, I just met her the one time. This is just dinner gossip my mother brings home. We have to listen to it every night."

"Don't knock it," Cora said. "She's got a good record of being pretty accurate. You might learn something valuable."

"She thinks she solves all the problems in this town." Amanda rolled her eyes. "I'll be sure and let you know as soon as she solves this case."

CHAPTER 24

"Mr. Dooley," Conrad said, stretching his arm out to shake Parnell Dooley's hand when he had been shown into his office. "I appreciate you seeing me today."

"How can I help you, Chief?"

Conrad took a seat in a leather tufted armchair that faced Parnell Dooley's large oak desk and looked around at the elaborate decor. "I didn't realize you were the president of the union when I was given your name as the local representative."

"Just of the local chapter," Parnell said. "We are a small part of a large regional and national organization. What can I do for you?"

"I'm told you were acquainted with Owen Hollingsworth. Is that true?"

"It is," Parnell said, clasping his hands on his desk. "He has been a member here for many years. He began as an apprentice and became a journeyman, training others in the craft. He also represents our union on the job site."

"He was active in your group? I'm told he attended meetings and was well acquainted with the workings of the union?"

"He attended meetings, yes. We hold meetings on the first Thursday of each month. He was present at most."

"Did you see him outside of the meetings? Outside of your offices here?" Conrad crossed his ankle over his knee.

"I have seen him at the work site."

"What about dinner? Did you have dinner meetings?"

"We don't serve dinner at the monthly meetings, although we do frequently have refreshments," Parnell said.

"Have you ever been to the Old Thyme Italian Restaurant to meet with Owen?" Conrad was taking a shot in the dark here, but Parnell's body language was guarded, and he was trying too hard not to say something.

"As I told your officer who telephoned me earlier, I haven't seen Owen recently. I last saw him at the work site when his supervisor was making unwarranted accusations that needed to be addressed. I attended a meeting with Owen and his supervisor to resolve that dispute."

"Okay, can you tell me a little more about that disagreement? How was it resolved?"

"His supervisor accused Owen of mishandling union property, some tools that the union had purchased. Owen assured him that he had not checked out those tools."

"Despite the fact that the sheet indicated Owen's name as the party requesting the tools," Conrad added. "I recall the reported theft."

"Yes. Well, it seems someone listed Owen's name because they must have had every intention of stealing the tool and didn't want to incriminate themselves."

"Hmm," Conrad cleared his throat. "Yet the procedure to checkout tools has not been changed. I admit I have thought that unusual."

"Well, that decision is at the discretion of the employer."

"Really?" Conrad straightened his back. "They are under the impression that changing the procedure requires union approval."

"We only ask for the opportunity to bargain," Parnell said with a smile. "They can propose changes to the procedure and then we negotiate."

"So, it's an act of Congress to make a simple change," Conrad said with a chuckle. "I can understand why the process remains inadequate."

"I think you are projecting your impatience at the wrong source, Chief Harris. What does this have to do with Owen Hollingsworth exactly?"

It was Conrad's turn to ignore a direct question. "What about Joe Barney? Or Josh Finley? Are they active members of your union?"

"They are both members, yes."

"Are they active? Do they come to meetings like Owen did?"

"I don't recall seeing them, but I'm sure they've attended before. Most members have at some time."

"Did Owen ever speak to you about Joe Barney?"

"What about him?"

"Let's start over," Conrad said, letting his foot drop to the floor to disrupt his irritation. "I am here to investigate the death of your union member, Owen Hollingsworth. I need for you to tell me everything you know about Mr. Hollingsworth. Your interactions with him, his work, his personal life, his concerns and his problems. I am sorting through a lot of observations and accusations surrounding his work and his involvement with the union and I'd appreciate your cooperation."

"I wish I could help you, Chief. I do. What little I know about Owen, isn't relevant to your investigation."

"You let me decide that." Conrad watched Parnell squirm under his stare and knew the man was withholding something. He had interviewed people for over thirty years, and he knew what a man with a secret looked like.

"I already told you," Parnell said, twisting in his chair to look at the glass window in his office door. "He was a good union member. He was well-liked and a capable journeyman."

Conrad glanced over his shoulder to follow Parnell's line of vision and saw a woman looking in the window. Conrad stood up when he heard the doorknob turn.

"Please, Chief, have a seat. I'm Malinda Grimes. I'm also an officer with the union. I hear you have some questions about Owen Hollingsworth. How can we help?"

"Well, I'm trying to ascertain what Owen's involvement was with the union and how it affected his relationship with Joe Barney. There was tension between them and with his boss, Alan Avery. All of this seems to be linked to his union affiliation. I know there is something significant here that I am not being told," Conrad said with a sharp glance toward Parnell. "It's important that I know the facts."

"I'm sure Mr. Dooley told you that Owen was an active member of the union and an excellent worker." Malinda Grimes sat down in the matching leather chair across from Conrad.

"He did." Conrad sat back and glared at Ms. Grimes. He hoped she realized that Parnell's information was inadequate. "Have you talked with Owen Hollingsworth, Ms. Grimes?"

"Oh, yes. He attends our meetings and has frequently been in the office. I'd say most everyone here is acquainted with him."

"What did you talk about? Recently, when you spoke with Owen, what was it regarding, specifically?"

"Oh, just union business. Nothing that would make any difference in your matter, I'm sure," Malinda said.

"It could make the difference between an innocent accident or a murder, Ms. Grimes." Conrad stood up and looked down at her. "As I told Mr. Dooley, you are not really in a position to make that decision for me. If I had more time, we could play this game of Ping-Pong all day, but I do have other obligations." Conrad moved toward the door. "Perhaps a meeting at my office would be more appropriate."

"Chief, we don't want to seem uncooperative." Malinda turned with her hands outstretched. "We were very fond of Owen and we want your investigation to be a successful venture."

Conrad put his hand on the doorknob. "I appreciate your positive thoughts, but I do require your candor as well. It can be given voluntarily, or it can be compelled by a court order. The choice is yours. Good day." Conrad tipped his head forward in a subtle bow and left the building with a knot in his stomach. There was something unsavory about these people. No one worked this hard to keep a secret that didn't matter.

§

Conrad pulled his squad car up and left it running as he entered the side door of the police station. "Briscoe!" Conrad called down the hallway. "We'll be back, Georgie. I'm going to the garage and then the construction site." Briscoe galloped down the hallway to the door.

"Okay, Chief," Georgia Marks called out from the dispatch booth where Briscoe had been curled up under her feet.

"Hop in, buddy."

Briscoe jumped in the driver's door and stepped gingerly across the center panel to the passenger's seat. He preferred riding shotgun to the perpetrator's backseat view.

Conrad parked on the side of the city garage and let Briscoe roam the area for a minute. The garage was on the west edge of town and surrounded by fields. Briscoe hadn't been out all morning and had never been to the city garage, so Conrad wanted to let him explore. Rodney Maddox ambled out of one of the open bays and waved.

"Hey, Chief. Is that the new officer?"

"Yeah," Conrad said, smiling. "That's Briscoe. He's checking out the place."

"I guess you want to check out the dumpster?"

"Yes. I think I need to take a look."

"Let me find the key," Rodney said, pulling a set of keys from his pocket and looking through them. "We've got it locked up down at the last bay. I need to warn you, though. It's starting to really smell in there." Rodney squinted as he held up the key. "I think that's it. Let me open it up."

Conrad watched Briscoe take in all the sights. His head pivoted sharply at the sound of the garage door opening and he ambled back toward Conrad. "Let's go check it out."

Rodney pushed the door up and waited to make sure it caught before swiping his palms together to dust them off. "There you go, Chief. You might want to give it a minute to air out."

Conrad stepped back and grimaced. Rodney had not been exaggerating, and Briscoe's nose bobbed up and down as he evaluated the situation.

Conrad pulled his flashlight from his pocket and, breathing through his mouth, he looked inside the empty cavern of the dumpster. Owen's presence had left a significant staining of blood and brain matter, as the reports indicated. The age of those stains diminished the coloring, but amplified the odor, and he kept his examination brief. The city garage may never be the same.

Briscoe lacked the height needed to peer into the dumpster, but he was sufficiently excited about the evidence bags on the worktable against the wall and the surrounding floor. Conrad looked through the items remaining and found many were not related to the construction site. Some effort had been made to separate out debris that appeared to have been disposed of by other vendors. There were broken down boxes clearly labeled as food items that would most likely have come from the Fennel Street Bakery.

Conrad had read the report of what had been shipped to the state lab for analysis but looked through smaller items gathered on the worktable. Small pieces of paper and wood, strapping tape and nails, and a circular saw blade. A small scrap of torn paper held a penciled phone number and Conrad photographed it with his phone. Grabbing the bag containing the saw blade, he snapped his fingers to get Briscoe's attention and walked back toward his car.

"You can lock it back up for me, Rodney."

"Sure, Chief." Rodney waved as Conrad backed his car out and turned towards town.

§

"I'm not doing this again." Parnell Dooley pushed his office chair back away from his desk as Malinda sat on the edge of the desktop.

"I don't understand why you're so upset."

"He knows we're involved, and we need to tell him what we know."

"He's just fishing around, and we both know that we don't have any information that will help him." Malinda slid off of Parnell's desk. "Don't be silly."

"I don't know that," Parnell shouted. "I don't know what happened down there. Maybe Owen got hurt because of what he was doing. You don't know that either."

"That's ridiculous. No one murdered Owen Hollingsworth because of a few tool thefts that no one even cared about. It's just bad timing."

"If he asks me again, I'm answering him. I'm not lying to the police."

"Nobody asked you to lie. They asked you to keep it quiet. Don't go blabbing it everywhere. We'll never find out anything if word gets out."

"Owen is dead. It's not worth it. I'm not going to court or getting arrested for keeping your secrets."

"My secrets?" Malinda said, pointing a finger at her chest. "This was all your original idea. Or have you conveniently forgotten that?"

"An idea, maybe," Parnell said, slumping back in his chair. "A bad idea that I wanted to end weeks ago, but you wouldn't let go."

"I'll handle the Spicetown Police. You just need to go on vacation for a while. Take some time off. Get out of town. Keep your mouth shut. I'll let you know when it's time to come back."

CHAPTER 25

"Hi, Connie," Cora said, testing the waters timidly when she answered Conrad's call.

"Hey, Cora. Are you busy?"

"No. I'm finishing up for the day. I'm sure you've had a busy day."

"I spent the morning reading reports and ran some errands this afternoon."

"Do you have time for dinner? I don't write reports, but I do have some information I need to share with you."

"I do," Conrad said. "I need to hear what you've learned so far. I don't want to duplicate effort."

"I'll warn you," Cora said. "Wink and I don't agree on a few key items, and I know you've only read his reports. He is pursuing things in a different direction."

"That's not all bad. Sometimes it offers the best coverage of the issues."

"Yes. I can see how that might help." Cora hoped Conrad had an open mind.

"I have some questions, but I don't need to interview everyone you've already talked to. You may be able to answer some of my questions."

"I hope so and I agree. No need to reinvent the wheel."

"Meet you at Old Thyme Italian?"

"Sounds great. I'll be there shortly," Cora Mae said as she pulled open her desk drawer to pull out her large satchel purse. Placing her maps and index cards in a folder, she wedged it into her handbag and grabbed her jacket.

§

"Hey there. It's Wink," Wink said in a rehearsed tone. He did not expect Mitzi to take his call and he had planned this voice mail message.

"I wanted to let you know that the Chief is back, and I'm getting ready to go to work, but things should go back to normal now. The Chief hasn't done the schedule yet, but I want us to go out of town and have a nice dinner on my first night off. I hope you'll talk to me again, and I want to see you real soon. Bye."

Wink stared at the phone in his hand and winced. He had messed up that whole speech. He should have written it down. He waited another minute, hoping the phone in his hand would ring right back. Maybe she'd listen and call him back giggling like she used to, but it didn't ring.

Wink called again.

"Hi, honey. I forgot to say something. You know I mess everything up. I hope you know that I'm sorry for upsetting you this week. It was a rough week for me. The Chief is mad and you're not talking to me.

Nothing went right, but what I forgot to say is, I miss you. I hope you miss me, too. Talk to you soon."

Wink tapped the button to disconnect and stared at the phone again. It just wouldn't ring.

Tossing the phone on the bed, Wink went to get dressed for work.

§

"So, you missed my cookin', huh?" Jo Anne Biglioni teased Conrad with her hand on her hip after he slid into a booth at the Old Thyme Italian Restaurant. Cora Mae hadn't arrived yet.

"Boy, did I! I didn't have a decent meal all week."

"Well, we'll see what we can do to fix that," Jo said. "Hi, Mayor."

"Evening, Jo." Cora pushed herself across the vinyl booth seat with a bounce.

"Here are the specials," Jo Anne said as she pointed to a chalkboard easel near their table and filled their water glasses. "I'll be back soon for your order."

"Thanks," Conrad said as Cora adjusted herself in her seat. "So? What have I missed this week?"

"Well, mercy! So much," Cora said, leaning forward in her seat and lowering her voice. "Charlene down at the sub shop got engaged to that boy from Paxton, and her mother is in fits. And Trudy got in a fight with Homer down at the Stop-n-Go and quit her job. Let me see, hmm. Eva Cantrell is back in the hospital. She just can't—"

"Cora, you know what I mean." Conrad rolled his eyes as Cora smiled innocently.

"Well, there's a lot more going on in this town besides just your little ol' case, Connie."

"And you've been to the beauty shop this week," Conrad said with a smirk. Cora Mae was always full to the top with trivia when she left there.

"I have. A fountain of knowledge."

"Okay, let's focus." Conrad cleared his throat when Jo returned for their orders and waited while she brought them their drinks. "You said on the phone that your direction differed from Wink's."

"Yes. Wink seems convinced that Joshua Finley is involved with Owen's death and I just don't agree," Cora shrugged. "He isn't following the flow of evidence. The phone in the dumpster doesn't incriminate Joshua. It excludes him."

"I agree. There are outgoing calls on his cell history from Sunday morning. He didn't lose that phone until Monday at work. I don't know how it got in the dumpster, but I don't see that it's related to Owen's death."

"Wink is also fixated on the trucks in the parking lot after five o'clock that Friday. I think that was just Owen and Alan talking. Owen would have left first, and the witness would have seen only Alan's truck left behind while he closed up."

"I have to say, my absence has given me a clearer perspective on Wink," Conrad said as he added cream and sugar to his coffee. "I'm disappointed, but it was information I needed."

"Wink is a good police officer."

"Oh, yes. I'm not saying otherwise. There's no one I'd rather have running patrol on the night shift. He's a capable leader, but Wink is not an investigator."

"Maybe he just needs some training," Cora suggested. "I could always ask the City Council for funding. We could see about getting him some formal training."

"I don't think that will do it. It wouldn't hurt, but I don't think that's his strength. He just doesn't think that way. He's not a puzzle solver. Does that make sense?"

Cora Mae nodded.

"He's an action guy. He sees a problem and he reacts. But thinking strategies and getting in other people's heads, it's not his thing."

"I have to agree. I had difficulty reasoning with him while you were gone."

"His reports were all over the place," Conrad shook his head. "There was no logic to what he pursued. Just stabbing in the dark. I've got some cleaning up to do to even make it flow."

"I have some drawings of timelines," Cora said as she pulled the folder from her handbag and pushed them across the table. "You ran out last night before I had a chance to give them to you."

"I couldn't deal with that last night. I was angry at Wink and I needed a good night's rest."

"So, what are your missing pieces? Maybe I have some answers."

"I don't have a clear picture on Owen and Joe Barney's relationship, and I think the union is hiding something, maybe about the both of them. Have you talked to them?"

"No, Wink said he had, but I did ask Alan Avery about them. I didn't realize how all of it worked."

"I'm pulling in Joe Barney in the morning. There are too many loose ends in his report, and I didn't find any follow-up to the reports that came in of Joe Barney walking on North Road or where his truck was that night. Wink didn't even explore any of that."

"Well, I've talked with Joe twice. His story was the same both times, but he has no alibi and he got a little testy with me the second time. You might want to get a formal statement from his ex-wife, too. I told Wink what Teresa told me when I called her, but I don't think he pursued it. She picked him up walking on North Road Friday night. She gave him a ride."

"Did you ask him about it?"

"I told him we had a report he was walking on the road. I didn't mention Teresa's name, but he denied it. I'm a little sorry I did that now, because he might think it's coming from Teresa. He was angry when I told him, and I don't want him angry at Teresa. Actually, Bryan is pretty confident that he saw him walking, too."

"I'll call her first before I pick him up tomorrow," Conrad said as Jo returned with plates in each hand.

"Here you go, Chief."

"That smells heavenly," Conrad beamed as Cora giggled. "I feel like it's been forever since I had a decent meal."

"Oh, the drama," Cora Mae smiled. "Thank you, Jo."

§

"Spicetown PD. How can I help you?" Sam Crawford twirled his chair around to grab a pen as he answered the phone in dispatch.

"Uh, hello. This is Parnell Dooley. I wonder if I could speak to Chief Harris?"

"Sure. He's not in right now, but I can have him call you. What's your number?"

"That's okay. Uh, I'll call back in the morning. Thank you."

"Sure thing. I'll let him know." Sam scribbled a message down for Conrad and tossed it in a stack as he reached to answer a radio call when Wink walked by the dispatch door.

"Is the Chief gone for the day?" Wink waited for his answer so Sam could finish his radio response.

"Yeah, Wink. He's gone, but we got a domestic call. You want to handle it, or should I send Hudson?"

"Go ahead and send Hudson. I'm going to grab some coffee before I head out."

"S9, Code 72 at 3419 Lemon Lane," Sammy said into his radio microphone.

"Who's the RP?" Wink asked over his shoulder as he turned to go to the break room for coffee.

"Teresa Barney," Sam called out.

Wink walked backwards a step from the door.

"She said her ex is drunk and banging down her front door."

Wink spun around to face Sam. "You need to notify the Chief. I'll head over there."

"Okay," Sam Crawford said as Wink strode briskly down the hallway and out the side door to his car.

§

"Do you feel better now?" Cora smiled as Conrad stretched back away from the table with a satisfied sigh and pushed his plate away from him.

"Yes, much better. I hope I never see another Blacktop Burger again." Conrad's forehead creased in a scowl.

"Is that what you ate all week?"

"They were next to the motel and had a drive-through. Briscoe wasn't really welcome anywhere, and I couldn't leave him."

"You know, he needs to learn to be alone at some point. During the day, he can hang out at the office, but you might want to go somewhere one evening—"

"And he can hang out at the office in the evening, just like he is right now." Conrad held up both hands in a shrug. "We're always open."

Cora Mae laughed. "Okay, I see your point."

"Sammy's calling," Conrad said as he glanced at his vibrating cell phone display. "Hey, Sammy."

Cora smiled up at Jo Anne Biglioni as she came to remove their plates.

"Is he all better now?" Jo whispered to Cora.

Cora Mae nodded as Jo carried the stack of plates away. "Thank you."

Conrad pocketed his cell phone and glanced around the room. "Teresa Barney called in a domestic. Says Joe is giving her some trouble. I think I'll drive over there. I need to talk to her anyway."

"Oh, I hope it isn't because of what I said. He may be blaming Teresa. I didn't even think when I said that to him." Cora grabbed for her purse and began scooting out of the booth.

"Doesn't matter. I was going to tell him myself if you hadn't."

"You go on. I'll get the check." Cora waved her hand to encourage Conrad to go. "You can get it next time."

Conrad nodded and pushed out the front door of the restaurant.

CHAPTER 26

"Hey, Chief." Wink was standing in the front yard of Teresa Barney's house when Conrad pulled in behind his cruiser.

"Could you turn off the lights on top?" Teresa yelled from her front porch. "My neighbors…"

"Sure," Wink yelled back as he walked to his car to turn off his blue light bar.

Darren Hudson was pushing Joe Barney into the back of his car and Teresa slipped into her house.

"Wink?"

"Yeah, Chief. Sorry." Wink walked back over to Conrad. "She's embarrassed. Joe's going to holding."

"Intoxicated?" Conrad waved to Officer Hudson as he slammed his back door shut on Joe Barney.

"Yeah, seems so. She wouldn't let him in."

"She okay?" Conrad asked.

"I think so. Just a little rattled." Wink motioned to Darren Hudson, who stood by his car. "You can take him in now."

Officer Hudson nodded and Wink pointed at Teresa's house. "I was going to get her statement."

"That's okay. I'll get it. I was planning to talk with her in the morning, but I can do both right now." Conrad opened his car door to grab his notepad that was in the seat. "I'll see you back at the station."

"Okay, Chief," Wink said as he hurried back to his car.

Conrad strolled to the front steps and Teresa opened the door as he reached the porch. "Evening, Mrs. Barney. Could I talk to you for a minute?"

"Sure, Chief. Come on in." Teresa held open her door and glanced around outside before motioning Conrad into her kitchen. "Can I get you something?"

"Oh, no. Just came from dinner," Conrad said, patting his stomach in appreciation of his warm meal. "I've been out of town recently and was planning to call you in the morning so we could chat. I thought maybe we'd just take care of all of it at once. What was going on here tonight?"

"I don't know. Joe never comes to my house."

"Oh," Conrad said, scribbling down the time and date on his pad of paper. "So, this is unusual."

"Yeah," Teresa said as she pulled out a kitchen chair to sit. "We've been divorced for six years. I rarely see him, and he never comes over."

"Do you know what he wanted?"

"He was yelling at me to open the door, but I could tell by the tone that it wasn't a good idea. I knew he must have been drinking."

"He's an angry drunk?" Conrad couldn't recall having previous domestic calls to the Barney house, but there might have been some years ago that he'd forgotten.

"He can be, yes. If he's mad about something, drinking will make it worse."

"What was he mad about? Have you two talked recently?"

"I picked him up when he was walking one night. He said his truck broke down and he paid me some back child support. We didn't fight or anything. He knows he owes me money, but I don't nag him about it."

"So, you don't know what he wanted to talk about tonight?"

"When he realized I wasn't going to open the door, he started yelling at me to keep my big mouth shut, but I don't know what he's talking about. He wasn't making any sense." Teresa ran her fingers up over her forehead and pushed her hair back. "I just told him to go home."

"Did you tell him you were calling the police?"

"No. When he kept yelling, I just called. I needed him to get off my porch before he disturbed all my neighbors. They're probably all peeking out their windows anyway. It'll be all over town tomorrow. You know how it is."

"Yeah," Conrad nodded. Spicetown was a friendly place where everybody knew your business. Little was ignored. "When was the last time he came to your house?"

"Years ago," Teresa said, leaning back in her chair and looking up over Conrad's head. "Probably about four years ago. He tried to.... My son doesn't really want to see him, but he did try to do things with him. He'd come by and invite him places, tried to get him to make plans with him, but he didn't want to go with his dad. Joe would get mad and yell at me about it, but I did everything I could to encourage a relationship. My son just doesn't want one. He finally gave up."

"Could tonight have had anything to do with your son?"

"Oh, no. They haven't talked in a couple of years. Joe doesn't even try and call him on his birthday anymore. I took him to court a couple of years ago for child support and he pays me when he can, but otherwise, we don't talk at all. I don't know what made him come here tonight. Maybe because he saw me recently, when I picked him up, and that opened a door to old anger issues. I have no idea."

"When you picked him up recently, do you recall what day that was?"

"It was Friday night, the sixteenth. I was driving home on North Road after I took Gloria Trent home from work. Her husband brought her in because her car was in the shop and I offered to take her home that night."

"You saw Joe walking when you were on your way back to town?"

"Yeah."

"Did you see his truck broken down somewhere? Or see him when you and Gloria went by?"

"No, I didn't see his truck anywhere."

"Did he say where he left his truck? Or tell you what he was doing out there?"

"No, and I didn't ask anything. I just asked him if he needed a lift to town and he got in. While I was driving, he said he had been meaning to send me some money and tossed some cash on the console."

"Does he usually pay you cash?"

"Never," Teresa said, shaking her head. "He only gets credit for it if it comes through the courthouse. I don't know what made him do that. I thought maybe he was just grateful that I stopped. It was getting dark."

"What time do you think it was?"

"I don't know," Teresa said as her eyes turned down to the tabletop. "We get off work at five o'clock, but we were a little late leaving. I stopped for gas first before I took her home. I'd say it was maybe close to seven. She lives way out there past Beck Farms on Marjoram Road."

"Where did you take him? Home?"

"No. He wanted me to leave him at the garage there on Chive Street. He said someone would still be there working and they would give him a ride to get his truck."

"Does he know someone there?" Conrad had seen this garage on Cora Mae's interview list, but he thought it was connected to the demolition derby pit crew workers.

"I don't know. I don't know much about Joe anymore." Teresa shrugged in apology, but Conrad understood that people grow apart and change.

"Was Joe in construction when you two were married?"

"Yeah, he has always done that type of work. When we were married, he was trying to get work on his own, so it was hit or miss. He joined the union right before we divorced, and I think that helped him. He got training and they found him jobs. I think he does all right."

"Did you know Owen Hollingsworth?"

"No, I never met him, but I knew he was Joe's friend. He met him when he joined the union and they worked together. He's mentioned him to me before."

"Was Joe worried about Owen's disappearance when you picked him up walking?"

"No, I mean, I don't really know if... When did that happen?"

"He was last seen at work on the sixteenth," Conrad said, glancing briefly at his watch. "I thought maybe Joe mentioned it to you when you gave him a ride that night."

"No," Teresa shook her head. "I didn't know about it then. I heard the next day when I went to get my hair done. The girls were talking about Owen there. They had heard he was missing, but that's the first time I'd heard it."

Conrad nodded. The rumor mill had elaborated again. "What had the ladies at the beauty shop heard?"

"Just that he was missing. I told them he was a friend of Joe's. Everyone just thought he'd left town or left his wife."

"Did you know Bonita?"

"No. I never met her, but Joe had mentioned her, too. He liked her. Some of the ladies at Louise's shop knew her. I think she gets her hair done there, too."

"Ahh," Conrad smiled. He saw plenty of opportunity there. "Did you mention to the ladies that you'd picked Joe up walking the prior evening?"

"Yeah, I did." Teresa paused and blinked. "You think that's what made him mad tonight? He thought I was talking about him?"

"You can't reason things out properly when someone drinks to excess. I wouldn't be concerned.

Have you seen Joe since you dropped him off at the garage?"

"I bet that's it. I bet someone in the beauty shop said I told them Joe was walking down the road. He wouldn't be involved in anything bad like that anyway. Owen was his buddy."

"Have you seen Joe since you dropped him off that night?"

"No. I haven't seen him or talked to him."

"If you do talk to him—"

"Oh, I don't plan to, not when he's angry. We don't really have any reason to talk anymore, anyway."

"Well, but if you do or you have any problems, please give us a call."

"I will, Chief, and thank you," Teresa said as she followed Conrad to the front door. "Is Joe going to be all right?"

"They took him back to the station. He'll sleep it off."

"Thanks, again."

§

"Morning, Fred," Conrad said as he strolled into the office. Fred Rucker was a part-time dispatcher that primarily worked weekend days and filled in when Georgie and Sam were off. He had handled dispatch for Spicetown for thirty years before he retired and then came back begging for work. He just didn't know how to retire. It was also one of Conrad's fears.

"Hey, Chief! Long time, no see. Hey there, Briscoe! He's not going to bite me now, is he?"

"Why would he do that? He likes you, Fred."

"Well, you went off and got him all trained now, so I figure he's too good for me," Fred said as he held out his hand to see if Briscoe would approach.

"He seemed to already know everything," Conrad chuckled. "They taught me a few things though." Briscoe approached to sniff Fred's fingers and then plopped down on his dog bed under the dispatch desk.

"Messages are on your desk, Chief," Fred said as he turned to answer the phone.

Conrad nodded and turned down the hallway to his office. His desktop was littered with reports from Saturday night and phone messages. Shuffling through the little green message slips he stopped and reached for the phone.

"Mrs. Barney? It's Chief Harris returning your call."

"Oh, hello, Chief. After you left Friday night, I realized I hadn't told you about Owen's wife calling me."

"Bonita? I thought you didn't know her."

"I don't. We've never met, but she called me that next day, the seventeenth, Saturday afternoon. She told me who she was and asked if I knew where Joe was. She explained that her husband hadn't come home, and she wanted to check with Joe. She thought he would have been with him the night before."

"What did you tell her?"

"I told her we'd been divorced for years and I didn't keep in contact with Joe regularly, but that I had given him a ride the night before."

"Was she alarmed? Or did she ask you anything else?" Conrad wasn't surprised that Bonita had reached out to Teresa. She had done her due diligence to locate Owen before calling in the police.

"She was upset that she couldn't find Owen. She was very nice, but I could tell panic was setting in. I didn't know how to help her. She seemed to know Joe really well and said he wasn't answering his cell phone. When I told her about picking him up Friday night, she did ask me why he was out on North Road. I thought that was kind of strange. I couldn't see any reason why she would need to know that."

"Hmm, maybe it just seemed odd to her. She may have expected him to be somewhere else Friday night."

"Yeah, I guess."

"Well, thank you for calling. I guess you haven't heard from Joe since his release Saturday morning?"

"Not a word," Teresa said. "Was he mad when left?"

"He left quietly. I tried to have a conversation with him, but he wouldn't talk to me. I would recommend that you not open your door to him if he shows up, though."

"Oh, I don't plan to. This whole thing now has my son angry and I hope Joe doesn't try to come around. I don't need the two of them to get in a fight about it. Joe wouldn't tell you why he came here or what he wanted?"

"No and he wouldn't talk about Owen either. He said he wanted an attorney and refused to talk. He has that right, so we let him go with a citation."

"Hmm, strange. Okay. Thanks, Chief."

Conrad agreed. He had questioned Joe about his whereabouts that Friday evening, the sixteenth, and rather than give the explanation he had previously given to Wink and Cora, he had refused to talk. When Conrad told him that there were multiple witnesses that saw him walking down North Road that evening, Joe had stared at the wall and would not confirm or deny. He had never explained where his truck was parked when he was seen walking and Wink's notes didn't indicate the question had been asked. A missed opportunity, and Conrad wished he had been here to handle the case from the beginning.

Conrad tossed the phone message from Paulie Childers of The Spicetown Star into his wastebasket. Wink had provided the paper with a prepared police statement and Conrad had nothing to add. Tapping his pen on the phone message from Ruth Hollingsworth, his desk intercom buzzed.

"Chief?" Fred said. "Erika Johnson is here to see you." Fred was the only one that used the antiquated intercom system. Georgia always ran down the hall and Sam Crawford just yelled. Fred didn't get up unless he had to.

"Send her back, Fred."

"Good morning, Chief." Erika stood in the doorway and Conrad rose from his seat.

"Good morning. Come in. Have a seat. I was just thinking about calling you today. I'm glad you stopped in."

"Oh, really? What about?"

"Well, I'll let you go first," Conrad chuckled. He didn't know Erika well and had usually spoken with Alan Avery when he had visited the work site. The reports Wink had gathered from both of them were sketchy and although he needed to talk to someone, he hadn't ruled out their involvement entirely.

"I have some concerns that I thought I should share with you. It may be nothing, but—"

"Of course," Conrad said, leaning forward. "About Owen Hollingsworth's death?"

"No, about all the thefts we've had since the project started. It's been really weird and maybe it's nothing, but I'm concerned that maybe Alan is involved somehow."

"Alan Avery?"

"Yes, he is, well, emotionally involved with the job. He got so upset about things involving Owen Hollingsworth. Owen's work quality and all the nuisance complaints he filed. I agree Owen has been a real pain on this job, but Alan just wasn't handling it well. He kept dragging Owen in and accusing him of leaving tools out and he thought Owen was stealing them. I was never convinced Owen had done any of it, and there's a small part of me that thinks maybe Alan was trying to find grounds to get Owen fired."

"But you've had a theft since Owen--," Conrad said.

"True, and maybe that one was legitimate. I don't know. I haven't told the company about my concerns because I don't want to jeopardize Alan's job if I'm wrong. I'm telling you because your officer asked me if I had any concerns and I couldn't really say anything at the time because Alan was sitting right there."

Conrad stifled a groan. Wink knew better than to interview that way. "I'm glad you're telling me now. I haven't had a chance to talk with Alan since I returned, but I planned to do that. Do you think the thefts were in any way related to his death?"

"Oh, no. Well, I don't see how. Have you found out anything about that?"

"We're working on it, but I'm glad you came in today. In light of what you've said, I would like to talk with you about an idea I had to catch your tool thief, but we probably shouldn't share this with Alan just yet."

"Really?"

"Yes, but I would need you to keep the information secret or the plan will not work."

"Of course, Chief. What is your plan?"

CHAPTER 27

Officer Eugene Tabor bumped his head on Erika's desktop when he crawled out from under her desk. "Reboot it again, Chief. See if it's working now."

Conrad pushed the button and waited. Erika Johnson sat at Alan Avery's desk in the tiny work trailer and watched.

"I'm getting a message box," Conrad said, and Tabor looked over his shoulder.

"Just click on okay," Tabor said. "That's it. See, there's Reynolds." Tabor pointed at the black and white display of Officer Adam Reynolds standing on the second floor of the community building in the hallway.

"Oops, it's gone," Conrad said as he shook the mouse back and forth.

"He has to move. It's motion activated."

"Move, Reynolds," Conrad barked into his radio and the screen popped back on to show Officer Reynolds walking in and out of the offices on the second floor. "Is it recording?"

"Yeah, it records when the motion activates it."

Conrad lifted his radio. "Come on down, Reynolds." Conrad saw him nod and walk toward the steps. The screen went black when he left the second-floor area. "It's not perfect, but hopefully it will catch whatever happens up there at night."

"It looks great," Erika said. "Do I need to do anything tomorrow night before I leave work?"

"Just stay a little late and let Tabor inside the trailer. He'll take care of everything from there." Conrad moved away from the laptop so Tabor could put things back in place."

"Everything working?" Officer Reynolds stepped inside the door and Conrad motioned him over to the table.

"Tabor can show you what you need to do." Conrad stepped aside to let Reynolds in and stood beside Erika. "Do you think you'll have any problems tomorrow? Does Alan usually work late?"

"No. One of us stays until everybody is off site, but I'll just tell him I have things to work on. He'll probably leave by five o'clock."

"When the coast is clear, call the office and somebody will drop Tabor off. Then when you leave, you can act like you're locking up, just don't lock him in. Okay?"

Erika chuckled. "Okay. I don't need to stay?"

"No. It will probably be pretty boring sitting in the dark. We may have to move it to the station if nothing happens in a day or two, but I'd prefer to have someone on the scene."

"I got it all, Chief," Tabor said as he picked up the laptop bag.

Conrad opened the trailer door and looked around before proceeding down the steps.

.

§

"Amanda?"

Amanda appeared in Cora's doorway with a stack of mail in her hand.

"Do you know why Ruth Hollingsworth asked me to call her? Did she say what she wanted?"

"No, she just asked if I would give you a message to call her."

Cora Mae groaned. "I can't imagine what it could be."

"You look like you're dreading it," Amanda said with a compassionate smile.

"I hate to say it, but I'm not looking forward to it. I know she is not one to be ignored. I guess I'll bite the bullet."

Amanda giggled and returned to her desk as Cora picked up her phone.

"Hello, Ruth. It's Cora Mae. You asked me to call?"

"Oh, yes, Cora. I wanted to ask you something. You know we spoke the other day about the annual book sale, and I told you we were having a storage problem. I wanted to see if you have any unused space at City Hall that we might use. A room, perhaps? Could we store some books in an office upstairs? We would free up the space for you as soon as the book sale is held. It would only be for a few months."

"I don't think we have any unoccupied space, Ruth. I can ask the council if they have any ideas, but the offices upstairs are taken by water department staff and the conference room is used regularly. Is your basement storage all full?"

"Yes, it's packed. That's why it is so urgent that we hold this sale. Do you have any updates on the community center yet?"

"No, Ruth. There's been no change." Cora shook her head.

"Well, I hope they are still on schedule."

"How is your sister-in-law doing?"

"Bonita? I'm sure she'll be fine. As far as I know, they haven't released Owen, so there haven't been any plans made."

"Have you talked with her?" Cora frowned at Ruth's insensitive tone

"Certainly. I told her to contact me if she needed anything."

"Well, you take care, Ruth."

Cora hung up the phone and let her shoulders slump as Amanda came around the doorway. "She's just worried about her book sale."

"I thought maybe she wanted to complain about her brother's case," Amanda said.

"No, she wouldn't even have mentioned it if I hadn't asked. She doesn't seem concerned that her brother has died at all."

"Maybe she's just covering up," Amanda said. "She has a reputation for being very stern and she doesn't want to show her feelings, so she doesn't talk about things that might make her emotional."

"You put a nice spin on it, dear." Cora winked at Amanda and smiled. She didn't believe it for a minute.

"Are they working at the construction site today? It's still raining really hard outside." Amanda walked to Cora's window and looked through the blinds. "Jimmy Kole said the trash people were supposed to pick up the dumpster from the city garage today but were afraid their truck would get stuck in the mud out there. They're going to leave it until it clears up some."

"We need to gravel that drive," Cora said, searching her desk for that list of future projects she kept. She jotted down a note so she would remember it for next year's budget. "I assume they are working today. I haven't been down there, but most of what's left to do is inside."

"Morning, ladies," Conrad said, tipping his hat at the door and watching the water fall from it.

"Connie, you're making a puddle. What are you doing out running around in this?"

"Places to go. People to see. A typical Monday morning." Conrad smiled as Amanda slipped out the door. "Mind if I shut the door?"

"Not at all. Have a seat," Cora said. "What are you up to today?"

"I wanted to let you know what was going on, but it's top secret. No beauty shop gossip."

"Now, you know I don't share things at the beauty shop," Cora said with a straight back.

"I know. I just mean none of this should be coming back from that source. I haven't even told Wink."

"He has a weakness in that area right now," Cora said with a raised eyebrow.

"I know, and I'm not done addressing that yet either."

"So, what's so secret?"

"Well, you remember that fancy high-tech stuff Amanda got for us last year with that grant money? It was a bunch of cameras that had all kinds of gizmos on it with infrared this and that. It was for night recordings and motion."

"Yes, I remember. Did you ever figure it out?"

"Tabor has. He understands all of that malarkey. Anyway, we hooked it all up yesterday on the second floor of your community center and around the parking area. Reynolds is going to sit up in the trailer tonight and keep an eye on the place. Maybe we can see where the tools are going."

"Wow, that's a great idea. Is it worth all the work, though? I haven't seen any evidence that they care much about the disappearing tools. They haven't tightened security at all, and I've asked about it more than once."

"I know, but I think it may tell us more than just where the tools are going."

"You think the thefts are linked to Owen?" Cora propped her chin in her hand. "I've never understood why the construction company didn't do this before."

"The tools have all been owned by the union, at least the ones that were taken," Conrad said as he crossed his foot over his knee.

"If something does happen, is Adam supposed to run up there and catch them at it?"

"It's all recorded. That's the beauty of it," Conrad smiled. "If he doesn't catch them at it, we still have the tape or whatever it is. Tabor said they don't use tape anymore."

"This will be interesting. I'm actually looking forward to someone stealing something now." Cora Mae laughed. "Isn't that awful?"

"You have to keep this quiet. Nobody knows, not even Alan Avery, so if you go down there, don't say anything to anyone."

"Are you going to tell Wink?"

"I guess I'll have to since he'll wonder where Reynolds is, but I don't plan to tell him until the very last minute."

§

"Wink, it's Mitzi. I know you're probably sleeping now, but I got your messages."

Mitzi drew in a deep breath and almost forgot the speech she had planned to leave on Wink's voicemail. She wasn't ready yet to talk to him and wasn't sure she wanted to give him another chance. The whole week the Chief was gone, Wink had treated her like she was an afterthought, something he would try to sneak in if he had time. She wasn't going to be mistreated anymore. She'd rather be alone than be with someone that made her feel unimportant.

"I'm willing to give this a second try, but don't make a date with me that you can't keep. If you aren't certain you can get through an evening without running out on me, don't call me back."

Deciding that was enough, she said goodbye and hung up. If he called, she would hold him to that commitment. If he didn't, maybe it was for the best.

§

Back at this desk, Conrad squinted at his long list of emails. He had tried to catch up over the weekend by opening the items that seemed significant, but a week's worth of nonsense was still sitting there. It was time to take it one by one.

Reading the coroner's report again, Conrad hit the print button and ran a search of his Inbox to highlight anything regarding Owen Hollingsworth. Working with a shorter list now, he opened and read each one.

An email from SpiceTel caught his eye. If it hadn't been for the search of Owen's name including it, he might have deleted it, assuming it was merely advertising from the local cell phone company. Attached to the email was a listing of all the incoming and outgoing calls on Owen's phone.

Owen's last call had been placed on Friday at 5:37pm. That would have been after he talked with Alan Avery so he might have just been reporting on that meeting, but Conrad had cause to ask.

Conrad grabbed the phone and called the work number that Parnell Dooley had given to him.

"Carpenters Union, this is Maggie. How can I help you?"

"This is Chief Harris of the Spicetown PD. Can I speak to Parnell Dooley, please?"

"I'm sorry Chief. Mr. Dooley is on vacation this week. I can transfer you to his voice mail if you'd like to leave a message."

"No. No thank you. When do you expect him back?"

"Next week, I think. Would you like to speak to Malinda Grimes? She could give you a better idea or she might be able to help you."

"No, thank you. Have a nice day."

Conrad looked at the number on the trace list and picked up the phone again. This cell phone number was registered to Parnell Dooley and not to the union, so it must be his personal number that Owen called that night. Conrad was not surprised when it was answered by a voice mail message.

"Mr. Dooley, this is Chief Harris. It's important that I speak with you. Your office told me you were on vacation and I hate to interrupt that, but please call me at the Spicetown PD. I have a few questions for you. Thank you."

Conrad glanced at the clock on his computer screen. He would give him 24 hours to respond.

§

Standing to stretch and growling out a yawn, Conrad strolled down to dispatch. All of his emails had been read and filed. He had learned little but was relieved the task was completed.

"Georgie, I'm taking a walk down Fennel. Briscoe needs to stretch his legs and I could use some air."

"Okay, Chief."

"Let's go, boy." Conrad slipped the leash off the hook by the door and Briscoe leaned against his legs while he clipped it on.

The air was cool for a late summer day, but the morning rain had introduced a hint that autumn was waiting in the wings. Conrad strolled to the light and crossed Fennel Street at the stoplight so he would be on the right side of the street to get to the construction site. A large moving van was parked on Fennel near the bakery and he wanted to see why.

Walking slowly so Briscoe could examine each parking meter, Conrad saw two young men wrestling with a long table in the back of the van while a third man was dragging a handcart of boxes through the front door of what used to be Ivy's Oils & Organics. The storefront had been vacant for months and although he had seen realtors show the property a few times, no business had moved in.

Pausing on the sidewalk, Conrad looked into the back of the truck and one of the men jumped down to the street, glancing nervously at Conrad and then Briscoe.

"Afternoon, gentlemen." Conrad gave the leash a slight tug and Briscoe sat at attention beside him. "Moving in?"

"Yes, sir."

"What kind of business are you opening?" Conrad glanced at the door when he heard the bell jingle.

Pushing an empty handcart, the approaching man stopped. "Is everything okay? Is it all right that we parked here? We'll have it all out in a few minutes."

"Sure. That's no problem. Just wondered what was opening up. What kind of shop are you boys opening?"

"We're just the movers," the young man behind the truck said. "I think it's a flower shop. The lady is inside."

"Hmm, I guess we need one of those," Conrad said, smiling. "Don't let me delay you." Tugging on Briscoe's leash again, Conrad walked by the bakery and down the street toward the construction area with a satisfied smile. He had actually found out something was happening in Spicetown before Cora did.

§

Wink listened to the voice mail from Mitzi when he woke up. He had a couple of hours before he had to be at the station, but he didn't know what to say to her.

He had planned to ask the Chief about his schedule and make sure before he talked to Mitzi because it was clear she was not going to tolerate any interruptions. The nature of his life really didn't allow for that promise, though. Even if he could get through one evening without getting called out or talking to one of the other patrolmen by phone, he couldn't promise it wouldn't happen again.

Mitzi may never be able to accept his life as it was. Looking back over his week as Acting Chief, he realized that Mitzi had caused him as much stress as the responsibility of the job had, and he hadn't successfully handled either one. As much as he wanted to spend time with her, he knew this just wasn't a good match for him.

Part of him wanted to make the promises she wanted to hear and deal with the fallout later when he couldn't keep them. That's the way he'd handled dating in the past. The other part just wanted to walk away and not call her back. He didn't really need the stress of an unreasonable obligation.

He decided to do nothing right now and see if he could find a compromise.

§

"Hi, Chief. Who's your friend?" Erika Johnson met Conrad as he walked up to the construction site and held out her hand to Briscoe. "Is he friendly?"

"Until I tell him not to be," Conrad chuckled. "How's it going today?"

"Pretty quiet," Erika said as she glanced over her shoulder when the office trailer door shut.

"Hey, Chief!" Alan Avery hopped down the metal steps and slapped his hard hat on.

"Alan," Conrad said with a tip of his head.

"I'm heading upstairs," Alan said to Erika. "Cy finished Barney's trim out and we'll be ready for paint tomorrow on the west side. The flooring should be delivered by 6:00 A.M."

"Good. I'll stay late tonight to close if you can be here for the delivery."

"Sounds good. See you later, Chief." Alan walked away and Erika smiled at Conrad.

"That worked out well. Since I have to drive from Paxton, Alan is usually here before me, anyway." Erika stroked Briscoe's head and scratched him behind the ears.

"Someone will drop Tabor off here as soon as you call the office to let us know everyone is gone. Hudson will have someone pick him up at 4:00 A.M. when his shift ends. If something is going to happen, I don't think anyone would risk doing it after that time."

"Okay."

"It sounds like you are nearing the end."

"Yeah. The main floor is going to take a few weeks, but the biggest piece is laying new flooring and we'll start that tomorrow. Joe Barney called in sick today. I'm not sure I believe him, but that almost caused us another delay. Cyrus McDaniels is a fast worker, though, and he was able to finish up Barney's part, so we're all good."

"Do you mind if we take a look around?" Conrad glanced down at Briscoe. He was looking curiously at the building and the bustle of activity around it.

"Not at all. Let me get you a hat," Erika said as she jogged up the steps quickly to the trailer. "I don't have one for your friend though."

"That's okay. He likes to live dangerously." Conrad laughed as he walked Briscoe toward the building.

CHAPTER 28

"How did it go?" Amanda smiled when Cora returned from her City Council meeting.

"Lovely, as usual," Cora said, running her hand through her hair again. It had been a frustrating meeting, but those stuffy old men would never learn. They were so determined to keep Spicetown behind the rest of the world that she had to work twice as hard to improve it.

"Did they pick a new name for the factory?"

"No, but there was much discussion about it. They didn't seem capable of agreeing on that, either. Larry Langley seemed fond of the name Allspice Community Center, and I understand the logic of that."

"I think I'd end up calling it the ACC," Amanda said and slumped her shoulders. "You can't call it The Allspice and the whole thing is just too much to say."

"I can see that, too." Cora dropped her stack of papers in Amanda's wire basket on the corner of her desk and lifted her leather binder. "I'm still considering The Spice Jar. It's nice and short, snappy. I don't think anyone would ever call it The Jar. Do you?"

"Um, I don't know. They might."

"I certainly don't want to hear that." Cora flipped through the pages in her binder. "Gordon Little mentioned just calling it The Spice Center, but that didn't grab me either."

"It's not bad," Amanda said. "It sounds like it's short for something longer, though. No one mentioned calling it the Spicer Center after our founder?"

"No, but this group doesn't like to acknowledge we have founders. That just dredges up the issue of the statue, and some of them aren't over that loss yet." Cora chuckled at the memory of her win.

"Did you like Laura's suggestion, One Spicetown Plaza? She had me add it to the list this morning."

"I prefer to have it sound like a homey warm place to congregate rather than a fancy city-style building." Cora flipped another page before closing the binder. "Right now, I'm sticking with the Spicetown Community Center until something better comes up. We still have some time."

"Did they give you trouble about the dumpster in the garage? Larry called and asked a bunch of questions about it a few days ago."

"Oh, yes," Cora said, rolling her eyes. "He complained, but I ignored it. He can't do anything about it. It's my decision and it's done." Cora went to her desk and Amanda followed. "There was something new that came up, which surprised me."

"Really? What was that?"

"There was a proposal made to annex the area north of town and that would affect Bryan. The cut off on the map was the north property line by Mavis Bell's house."

"Wow," Amanda said. "Who requested that? And why?"

"It's a company called Redding Realty, Inc. They bought a large piece of property and want to subdivide out there, but they want to be in the city limits. I'm assuming so they can get Spicetown water."

"Is that a good thing?" Amanda scrunched her nose. "Are you in favor of it?"

"I'm not sure yet. We tabled it for now and I'll have to do some research on them. They aren't a local company and I don't know who runs it. I guess it could increase our revenue, but it would also make us responsible for more road maintenance and street lighting. We'd get tax money from Bryan and the other businesses out there, but it might not offset our costs. I just don't know yet."

"Can I mention it to Bryan? I don't know that he'd care other than I guess he'd need a business license."

"You can tell him. He would have to collect and remit city taxes and get a license, but he'd have a better-quality road coming out to his business."

"He'd have more people building houses out there, too." Amanda said. "That could mean more landscaping jobs for him."

"True," Cora nodded. "Seeing Spicetown grow is always a positive to me, unless it is filling up with the wrong people. I'll have to check these folks out."

"Mayor?" Harvey Salzman peeked in the doorway.

"Hey, Saucy. Come on in. I saw you at the meeting. We were just talking about the proposed annex."

"Oh, yes. That was a surprise. Did you know about it?"

"No. It surprised me, too. I haven't seen you at a meeting in while. Did you come for a special reason?"

"I was just being nosy," Saucy said with a smile. "I thought I'd hear more about the community center. I was curious how it was coming along."

"Everything seems to be on schedule. I still expect to have a grand opening in October. Did you submit a name for the center?"

"That's one of the reasons I thought I'd stop in. You didn't seem too taken with any of the suggestions," Saucy said as Amanda slipped by him in the doorway to answer a ringing phone.

"Not yet. I'm still thinking about it," Cora said, picking up the list she had distributed at the meeting.

"The other thing was the new business in town. I was curious about that and it didn't even come up."

"New business? I didn't know we had a new business in town. Where is it?"

"Right there on Fennel Street," Saucy said with raised eyebrows. "You didn't know?"

"I didn't. Amanda," Cora yelled. "Did you know we had a new business in town?" When Amanda didn't return, Cora shrugged. "She must be on the phone. What do you know about the business, Saucy?"

"Just that it's a flower shop and it's going in the place where Denise Ivy had her store. They're moving in today, but I don't know when they plan to open."

"Well, I'll be! I can't believe I hadn't noticed that. They must not have a business license yet."

"There's not a name up on the front, but the movers told me it was a flower place. We don't have one anymore since Mabel retired. I think we probably need one. Don't you?"

"I sure do. It sounds like a lovely idea. I wonder who it might be. I'll be sure and let you know as soon as I hear."

"Thank you, Mayor. It's time I get on home now. It's getting dark earlier every day." Saucy turned to go and waved at Amanda.

"Wait, Saucy," Cora called out.

"Mayor?"

"You didn't tell me what you think of the community center names. Do you have a favorite?"

"Well, I wasn't thinking of anything fancy. I thought The Spicetown Welcome Center would be a nice name and maybe people would stop there as they came into town. I guess that sounds like a rest stop instead of a civic center, though. I didn't actually submit the name. It's just the way I've always thought about the place since you started on it."

"Saucy, that's brilliant. I love it! Amanda!"

"Yes?" Amanda returned to Cora's room with a note in her hand.

"Saucy has just given us a wonderful name. What do you think of The Spicetown Welcome Center? We could have pamphlets in the lobby so people could learn about our town history and maybe a map of the town. Even a little book about spices! We're going to have someone there every day in the office. There's no reason we can't encourage people coming into the town to stop there. It's the first thing they see if they're coming from the west."

"That sounds great, Mayor," Amanda said as Saucy smiled shyly.

"Let me get going, ladies," Saucy said, waving to them over his shoulder. "I'll see you both later. Have a good evening."

"Bye. Take care." Cora waved back when Saucy glanced over his shoulder.

"I really like that. It's got a warm feeling to it."

"Oh," Amanda said, thrusting the note in her hand. "The Chief called and said he can't make dinner at The Barberry Tower tonight but said he would call tomorrow and maybe you could have lunch."

"Great. Thank you. I haven't heard from him in a few days. I hope he's got some news on Owen's case."

§

"What's the latest on your love life, Mitzi? Are you still dating Wink?" Mitzi looked in the mirror and met Darlene's eyes as she combed Darlene's wet hair.

"I don't know. We had a little bump in the road last week and I don't know where we're headed."

"That's a shame. What happened?" Louise piped in from the chair next to Mitzi's station.

"I know last week was busy for him with the Chief being gone and I got a little impatient. I gave him an ultimatum and he's not called me back." Mitzi ran her fingers through Darlene's hair to apply some conditioner before her blowout.

"Some men run from ultimatums," Darlene said with a grimace. "He's got an important job, and last week was especially hectic."

"Finding Bonita's husband in the dumpster with the Chief out of town..." Louise winced. "It was probably a bad time to start a relationship."

"I know," Mitzi said, shaking her head. "I know it was a bad time and maybe I'm being unreasonable, but I just refuse to be disrespected anymore. I've had that and it's better being alone."

Louise glanced at Darlene in the mirror as they exchanged knowing looks.

"Well, I hope you don't have to settle for either one," Darlene said as Mitzi turned on the blow dryer.

§

"Hey, Alan. Got a minute?"

"Sure, Barney. What's up?"

"I wanted to tell you that I'm movin' on this weekend. You'll need to call and get a replacement for me." Joe Barney took a seat in the chair across from Alan Avery's desk in the construction site trailer.

"Really? Okay. Where are you headed?"

"Heading south before it gets cold. I got a new job near Atlanta. It should give me work through the rest of the year."

"Wow. Sounds like a good deal. You're leaving out this weekend?"

"Yeah, gotta be there Monday." Joe Barney got up and walked to the door.

"Hey, Barney. Is Owen's wife doing okay? Have you talked to her at all?"

"Not really. I know I should, but I'm not good at that stuff. You know?" Joe reached for the doorknob.

"Yeah, I know, but she seems like a nice lady and that was really awful. I hope the union is taking care of her. Insurance and all."

"I'm sure they are," Joe scowled. "Owen was a big union guy. They ought to take care of her."

"Well, if you see her before you go, please tell her that she can call me if she needs anything."

"Yeah, I will," Joe said with a half wave as he pushed open the trailer door and left without looking back.

CHAPTER 29

"I already know what I want." Conrad rubbed his stomach.

"We haven't even sat down yet," Cora scolded.

"I went a whole week without food, remember?"

"Oh, that. You can't keep using Kentucky as the excuse," Cora said, smacking Conrad's upper arm with the back of her hand. "Let's sit in the front window. What are you going to have?"

"They have the catfish plate on special."

"Hey there! Tea and coffee for you?" Dorothy Parish handed out menus as she walked by. Dorothy had owned the Caraway Cafe on Fennel Street for years.

"Yes, please," Cora said as Conrad nodded.

"Have you checked out the new business?" Cora pointed across the street to the vacant storefront that was beginning to show a few signs of life.

"I've not been inside yet, but I saw them moving in the other day. The movers said it was a flower shop and there is a woman running it."

"That's more than I knew. Saucy told me it was a flower shop, but they haven't applied for a license yet."

"I was hoping to beat you to the scoop," Conrad laughed. "You always hear everything before I do."

"That's not true. I haven't heard a thing about Owen Hollingsworth all week. What's going on with your little secret?"

"That has been a bust. I really thought we'd get something, but we've been out there four nights now and the only thing that has been recorded is a visiting squirrel."

Cora giggled and leaned back as Dorothy brought their drinks over to the table.

"What can I get ya?" Dorothy propped her ticket book up, ready to write.

"I'll take the catfish," Conrad said.

"And I'll take the chicken salad plate." Cora shut the menu and handed it back to Dorothy.

"Any news on when the factory is going to be done?" Dorothy asked Cora. "We're not in any hurry now, but I was just curious. We kind of like the boys coming over here for lunch through the week."

"Just a few more weeks, I think," Cora said.

"Have you met the new folks setting up shop across the street yet?" Conrad pointed out the window.

"Nope, not a word yet. I saw some movers, but I don't know who they are." Dorothy grabbed Conrad's menu. "I'll get your tickets in."

"Thanks, Dorothy," Cora said as she stirred her tea until Dorothy walked away. "Have you been over to the construction site today?"

"No. I was there yesterday and talked to Erika for a minute."

"Well, I just came from there and I talked to Alan. He said Joe put in his notice this morning." Cora stared at Conrad. "He told him he had a job in Atlanta and was heading out of town this weekend."

"They only give one day's notice?" Conrad huffed.

"Well, Alan didn't seem alarmed. Maybe it happens all the time. I don't know. He said he'd just call the union and they'd send someone in his place Monday."

"I'm alarmed," Conrad said, straightening his back. "I don't want him leaving town right now."

"I thought you might feel that way."

§

"Wink!" Officer Hudson yelled out in a whisper when Wink answered his cell phone. "I got movement on the second floor. One male."

"I'm close," Wink said, turning his car around. "I'll cover."

Officer Darren Hudson had camera duty tonight and he'd been told to keep it off the radio. Wink didn't have time for that now and called Officer Adam Reynolds over the radio and directed him to the construction site for an assist.

As he pulled into the lot and jumped out of his car, Wink saw Hudson coming down the stairs of the old popcorn factory pushing Joe Barney in handcuffs in front of him.

"Male in custody," Wink said into his shoulder radio.

"Copy," Sam Crawford said from dispatch.

Wink opened his back door as Darren Hudson pushed Joe Barney into the backseat of Wink's squad car and slammed the door. "You gonna call the Chief?"

"No. Just putting him in holding until morning."

"I've got to go in and get the laptop and lock up," Hudson said as Wink opened his car door.

"Did he say anything to you?" Wink waved at Hudson to pull up beside him.

"Not a thing and no resistance at all. I didn't catch him with anything on him though, so we may just have trespassing."

"That's enough to lock him up for the Chief. Good job."

"Thanks. I'll catch a ride back with Reynolds." Hudson walked around to Officer Reynolds window and told him he was locking up as Wink drove Joe Barney to jail.

§

"Good morning, Mr. Barney," Conrad said as he entered the interview room.

"Chief," Joe said with a nod of his head. Clasping his hands on the table, he stared at his hands.

"Can you tell me what you were doing in the community center early this morning?" Conrad dropped his head, trying to meet Joe Barney's eyes.

"I don't have anything to say, Chief."

"You were there to take tools. You've been skimming them during the whole project. What are you doing with them? Selling them?"

Joe Barney didn't look up but shook his head.

"Joe, save yourself and tell me where you're fencing them," Conrad said. "I'm sure they can't be any use to you unless you can liquidate them."

"I don't have anything to say, Chief."

"Why would you take the fall for petty theft? Why do you want to ruin your future, lose your new job? Just to cover for a fence? It's not a big deal."

Joe stared straight down at his hands on the table and Conrad decided to take another avenue.

"Okay. How are you getting the tools? They are locked up at night in the job box and they aren't left out on the floor. How are you getting them? You were signing them out under Owen's name, but you can't do that any longer." Conrad shifted in his chair. "Owen isn't around to take all the blame for what you're doing, is he? Who are you going to place the blame on now? How are you going to keep from having fingers pointed at you?"

"Just doing what I'm told, Chief."

"Ah, you're a puppet! Someone is telling you what to do? You're being coerced? You can't say no? I hope you're getting a decent cut. You'd have to steal a lot of tools to make any real money if you're sharing the profit. Is life that rough?"

Conrad paused and stared at the top of Joe Barney's head. His shoulders slumped and his gaze lowered.

"Who is your leader? Who is pulling your strings?"

"It's not like that," Joe said, slowly raising his head. "Nobody tells me what to do."

"Oh, so you just decided to steal from your own union. Was Owen helping you and now you don't have a partner to protect you? Now you're getting caught."

Joe shook his head and forced a fake chuckle as if Conrad was not even close.

"How are you getting the tools, Joe? Let's start there. The tools are locked up. You have a key. How did you get it?"

"Avery," Joe raised his head up to look directly at Conrad. "I got my key from Avery."

"Explain it to me," Conrad said, sitting back and crossing his ankle over his knee. "What's in it for Avery? Why would he give you a key or want you to take union tools?"

"He wanted to get rid of Owen." Joe threw out his hands and shrugged. "I tried to help him."

"And last night? Who was supposed to take the fall last night? No pun intended."

"That was different," Joe said, breaking eye contact.

"What did you do with the tools you previously lifted?"

"Sold 'em."

"Sold them to whom?" Conrad's foot dropped to the floor and he leaned forward. "The union?"

"I got nothin' else to say, Chief."

"Okay. I'll do the talking. Let me tell you how it looks to me. You were stealing tools and implicating Owen. Somewhere along the way, Owen found out what you were doing to him and you two fought at the work site. You pushed Owen to his death. Sound about right?"

"What? No!" Joe tried to jump out of his chair but was yanked down by the restraints. "That's not right. I want a lawyer."

"I would highly recommend that," Conrad said, pushing his chair back to stand. "If I've gotten something wrong, please feel free to correct me."

"I had nothing to do with Owen."

"You just told me you were stealing because of Owen. He was right in the middle of it. Either he was in on it and helping you, or he caught you and tried to stop it."

"I'm not talking," Joe said, bouncing his cuffed feet under the chair. "I want an attorney."

Conrad looked down at Joe Barney and walked to the door without another word, locking him in the interview room.

"What do you think, Chief?" Tabor had been watching the interview through the one-way glass.

"I don't think he's going to talk. The problem is, I don't really have anything to hold him on. I'm afraid if I let him go, he'll run to Atlanta or somewhere I can't find him, and I think I'm going to need him around."

"You can't hold him on the thefts?"

"I can't even hold him on *this* theft. He didn't have anything on him. It's a simple criminal trespass charge." Conrad grabbed his empty coffee cup he had left sitting outside the interview room.

"You can lock him up for the weekend at least. He can't get before a judge until Monday."

"Yeah. Let's just do that for now. I really need to talk to Parnell Dooley, and we keep missing each other. He's supposed to be back in town today and I need to see him. I think he's the missing piece."

"You want me to take him back to holding?" Tabor looked in the window and saw Joe Barney tapping his fingers on the table.

"Yeah. Just lock him back up for me. Thanks."

CHAPTER 30

"Mr. Dooley. I appreciate you coming in today. A lot has happened this week while you've been on vacation, and I do have some questions for you." Conrad sat down at the table across from Parnell Dooley and placed a notepad on the table.

"I'm sorry, Chief. I didn't mean to inconvenience you or anything." Parnell Dooley crossed and uncrossed his legs as his eyes roamed all over the room. "Malinda was available at the office. I'm sure she would have been happy to help you."

"I don't think so. What I'm most concerned with is your personal involvement and I wanted to get that information firsthand." Conrad had debated whether to use his office or the interview room for the meeting and had decided the environment of the interview room would be more unsettling to Parnell.

"I don't think I understand what you mean."

"Mr. Dooley, I need to know what deal you had with Owen Hollingsworth. I know you met a few times for dinner, and I know you were the last person he spoke to on the phone right before his death. I know those two things are related, so it's time now to tell me about it."

"I don't really have anything to tell, Chief. I mean, Owen was a good union member. He was interested in a job with the union and we talked about it. That's all."

"A job with the union?"

"Yeah, in the office. He was hoping the union might hire him. We talked about that."

"And what did you tell him? What did he need to do to have a chance at a union office job?"

"Nothing specific. He wanted to encourage membership and participate in membership drives. Maybe teach some classes. That kind of thing."

"And would that get him a job at the union?"

"Well, it could go a long way. I told him I thought it would put him in a favorable light when the regional office was hiring."

"I see," Conrad said. "So, you encouraged him?"

"Sure. I'd have loved to see him join our staff. He was very positive and upbeat. I think he would have been a good recruiter."

"Would it help him out with the job if he gave you information about members who were not doing well? If he had coworkers, other union members, who were not following rules or not performing well and he told your office about them, would that be viewed favorably?"

"Sure. We'd want to know. If someone needed additional training, we would make sure they got it."

"Okay," Conrad said, shifting in his chair as he shifted the topic. "Can you explain to me about how the union handles the tool purchases for the job site? Do you have a collection of tools that you loan out to each job as needed?"

"Oh, we don't provide everything, but we do have some of the more expensive items that aren't used every day. We provide them if they're needed on a particular job, but the carpenters provide their own hand tools and belt. The contractor provides safety gear."

"Who pays for the tools?" Conrad shook his head and frowned.

"The cost is shared. When a worker joins the union, we give the apprentice a tool list of things they are expected to provide, and the list grows when they become a journeyman. Contractors have their own list and sometimes there's a shortfall. We bridge that gap for our members."

"Hmm, where do you get your tools?"

"The same way anyone does," Parnell said with a shrug.

"How did the union handle the losses they've had from this job? There have been a number of tools stolen."

"That's true, but the tools are insured. Malinda might be able to give you more detail on this topic."

"If I recall, the dovetail saw was stolen first. Have you replaced it?"

"I believe so," Parnell said.

"Do you ever buy used tools, or do they all have to be brand new? I mean, if one of your union members needed some cash, would you buy a tool from them?"

"Perhaps," Parnell shrugged. "It would be checked out, and we would make sure it was in good condition."

"Of course," Conrad said. "Do you record your equipment by serial number or label them in some way to indicate they are union property?"

"Not to my knowledge. We have inventory of the items by make and manufacturer, of course."

"Has Owen Hollingsworth sold any tools to the union?"

"Not that I recall, but Malinda would be a better source for that answer."

"What about Joe Barney? Has he sold you tools?"

"Chief, I really have to refer you to Malinda for these issues. This is not something I handle. Are these questions in relation to the thefts or to Owen's accident?"

"Mr. Dooley, I'm perplexed by these methods. What would stop a union member from stealing tools on the job site and selling them right back to the union?" Conrad leaned forward and stared at Parnell as his eyes looked away in a daze. "I don't need Malinda for that. I'm speaking theoretically."

"Oh, well, uh, nothing I suppose."

"Do you keep records on who you buy tools from? Surely you must have records on these purchases."

"I'm sure we must."

Conrad made a note on his yellow pad to subpoena those purchase records. "Mr. Dooley, we suspect Joe Barney was stealing the tools. In fact, we have video of his attempt and he is currently here in jail."

"Oh, my. I had no idea."

"We also believe that Owen Hollingsworth was aware he was doing it and confided in you. What did Owen tell you about Joe Barney?"

"No, Owen didn't speak about the tools with me. He did tell me he had concerns about his friend, Joe. He had trained Joe in his early years, and he was concerned that he was not performing the quality work he had once done."

"And did you or someone at the union contact Joe Barney about this issue?"

"I don't know."

"Your story is not matching Joe Barney's story. Can you get me copies of all your purchase records today?"

"Uh, no. I don't have the authority for that. You would need to speak with Malinda on Monday. I've not—"

"I thought you were the president of this local," Conrad said. "Why is it that Malinda runs everything?"

"She's with the regional office. If she were not stationed here, I would have to wait until Monday to get approval from the regional office."

"You can't reach her right now?"

"Uh, I don't know." Parnell pulled out his phone from his shirt pocket and looked at the display.

"How about this," Conrad said as he stood up and pushed in his chair. "I'll step out and let you call her. If she's unable to provide the records today, I'll get the county attorney to issue a subpoena for them and we'll collect them that way. Considering Owen was your union member, I would hope you would want to give your full cooperation in the investigation. It looks better in the press that way, but the decision is yours. I'll be back shortly."

Parnell nodded and scrolled through his contact list as Conrad stepped out of the room.

§

"Wow, Chief. Did Barney tell you he was stealing tools and selling them right back to the union?" Tabor had been glued to the one-way mirrored window.

"No. Barney didn't tell me anything, really. He tried to implicate Alan Avery, but never mentioned the union. It just seems logical to me. What do you do with stolen tools? There's no fence around here for them and they aren't in great demand. You have to turn them into money some way."

"Maybe he sold them online."

"That's possible. Check on that for me. Georgie has the list of the stolen items. See if any are listed online for sale in this area. I just thought it sounded like a good idea to me. I mean, if I were a worker and knew the union would buy used tools from me, I can see someone doing it. That's why I need their records."

"Chief," Georgia Marks stepped out of the dispatch office and held out two phone messages. "The mayor called, and Mrs. Hollingsworth called. Both said it was nothing urgent."

"Hmm," Conrad glanced at the notes and turned to walk down to his office to warm up his coffee. Conrad had a special blend of coffee and a personal coffeepot in his office that no one was allowed to use. After adding a touch of cinnamon, he picked up the phone on this desk and called Cora while the water heated.

"I got a message you called."

"Hi, Connie. Yes, I just wanted to check with you first. I was planning to go over and visit Bonita Hollingsworth, but I didn't want to do that if I would be in the way or it would cause a problem. Her sister-in-law is not helping her with anything, and I wanted to make sure she didn't need something. I saw Alice Warner last night when I was shopping in Paxton and she said Bonita hadn't returned their calls. The coroner's office is ready to release the body, and she needs to make arrangements."

"It won't be any problem. Bonita called here, but I haven't called her back yet. Maybe she was calling with questions about the coroner's office."

"If that's the case, I'll help her make arrangements," Cora said.

"One other thing, we arrested Joe Barney early this morning at the construction site."

"Oh, really! Was he stealing tools?"

"Not technically," Conrad said. "He was on the second floor and the camera caught him, but he didn't have any tools when we arrested him. We're just holding him on criminal trespass, but the judge will probably cut him loose Monday."

"If it wasn't to take something, why would he be there?"

"I don't know. He's saying Alan Avery put him up to it. I'm going to have to talk to Avery again."

"Poppycock!" Cora huffed. "I don't believe a word of that."

"He said Avery wanted to get something on Hollingsworth and gave Joe access to the tools."

"Now, why would Alan go to Owen's best friend to set something up? If you wanted to do that, you'd find someone that hated Owen and that would also benefit from Owen being fired. Wouldn't you?"

"Yeah," Conrad agreed.

"Alan would risk Joe telling Owen and the whole thing blowing up in his face. Alan would lose his job! He's far too responsible to do something that risky."

"Perhaps," Conrad said. "Let Bonita know that I've gotten her message, but I probably won't get back to her until later today. I've got the union up here now too, so several interviews to tie up today."

"I will, and I'll let you know what she needs. Talk to you later," Cora said.

Conrad picked up his coffee cup and headed back down to dispatch. "Georgie?"

"Yeah, Chief?"

"Can you call Alan Avery for me? Ask him to come in the office today. I've got a few questions."

"Sure, Chief."

Conrad tried to get a quick sip, but it was too hot and left his coffee on a table near the interview room before opening the door.

"Mr. Dooley," Conrad said, pulling out a chair from the table. "Did you have a chance to get some answers?"

"I spoke with Malinda. She said she would be happy to comply with a subpoena."

"Ah, so she isn't interested in voluntarily cooperating. We will need to force the issue?"

"Appears so," Parnell said, looking down regretfully. "Chief, I wish I could tell you what's going on with all of that, but I just don't know. Malinda doesn't tell me everything."

"I see. That's a shame. I'm sure it is very demoralizing to be president and know you should be in charge of your office and staff, yet not be empowered to make even the smallest decisions. I can certainly understand how frustrated you must feel. Has it always been that way?"

"Oh, no. I've been there for three years and really enjoyed my job. Malinda just joined us in February, but she has made some significant changes."

"It seems one of those changes was to take away your office. She seems to control the place now."

"Yes," Parnell said, looking down at his clasped hands. "Sometimes it does."

"You seem to care about your union members and believe in what you do. That's why I—"

"Oh, I do, very much," Parnell said.

"That's why I expected you would want to contribute to our investigation, especially of Owen Hollingsworth's death."

"What can I do?" Parnell held out his hands in a helpless shrug. "I don't know what happened."

"Well, I assume Malinda told you that you could not give me the purchase records today," Conrad said as Parnell nodded. "But did she say you couldn't look at them and tell me what they said?"

Parnell's lips parted as he glanced to the side. "Would you like to run over to the office with me right now?"

"Sure, let's go," Conrad said as they both jumped up from their chairs.

CHAPTER 31

"Well, aren't you a busy bee this morning!" Cora lunged to catch the screen door as Bonita Hollingsworth dragged a box over the threshold of her front door and pushed it to the side of the porch. Glancing inside, she saw open boxes everywhere. "Are you moving out?"

"Oh, yes. Thank you, Mayor," Bonita said, pushing her bangs back from her forehead with the back of her hand. "This house is too much for me now that Owen is gone."

Cora thought the two-bedroom pillbox bungalow a rather modest abode. "Do you have somewhere new to go?"

"I do," Bonita said, stepping inside. "Please come in. Can I get you something to drink? I still have cups I haven't packed--"

"No. No, I don't want to be a bother. I just came by to see if you needed anything. I talked to the Chief this morning and he said you had called. I thought maybe it was something I could help you with. We didn't realize you were moving. Are you leaving Spicetown?"

"Yes. I don't have anyone here for me now."

"Where are you moving? Are you moving closer to family?"

"I'm moving to Atlanta. My sister is in Florida, and I may go there later, but I am going to Atlanta today for the winter. I do not like snow and the winters in Ohio are so hard for me. I grew up in Puerto Rico and we did not have this cold."

"Joe Barney is going to Atlanta, too. Did you know that?" Cora sat down on the end of the couch.

"Yes, I am going to follow him. I've never been to Atlanta, and I'm afraid of the driving there."

"Joe won't be leaving today, I don't think," Cora said as Bonita sat in a chair across from her. "He was arrested last night."

"Arrested! Why? Why would they arrest Joe?"

"I don't know all the details, but he was arrested on the construction site in the early hours this morning. I don't know why he was there. Do you?"

"Oh, his heart is hurting," Bonita said, wringing her hands. "He came by last night and we talked a long time. He feels very bad about Owen's accident. He misses him."

"His accident?"

"His fall, yes." Bonita nodded. "They were good friends and he wants to help me. When he said he was going to Atlanta, I knew that would be a better place for me, at least for a while. I really don't know anyone here but Joe."

"What about Owen's family? They are here."

"Ugh, just Ruth and she doesn't like me. She told me to stay out of things and she would handle it. She is one of the reasons I want to leave."

"Oh, I'm sorry to hear that," Cora said, shaking her head in mock surprise. She had hoped Ruth would be the one to stay out of things since she showed no concern for her brother. "I know the coroner is waiting to hear from you. They need to know what your plans are for Owen. Are you working with someone on that? Do you need help making arrangements?"

"Ruth is doing that. She did not like my plans and told me to leave it to her. I wash my hands of Ruth and all of it." Bonita swiped her palms together.

"But what will you do in Atlanta? Joe, I think, has a job there, but if you don't know anyone there either..."

"I will know Joe," Bonita said with an exaggerated nod. "That is enough."

"Well, the arrest might have changed things for him. He might not make it to Atlanta for his new job."

"They will let him out, won't they? He didn't do anything wrong. Owen's accident was not his fault. He told me so, and I believe him."

"What exactly did he tell you?" Cora scooted to the edge of the couch with a furrowed brow.

"He told me they argued. He felt so bad about it. They almost never argue, but Joe said he was angry with Owen and they fought. When Owen fell, Joe did not know what to do. He knew Owen was hurt too badly, that calling someone would not help him. He knows he should have but he got scared and he had to get away. He couldn't talk about it then. He just left."

"He left in Owen's truck. Why would he take Owen's truck?"

"I don't know," Bonita said and then smiled. "I didn't ask him that."

"I... I'm surprised. You seem so at ease with this. You're not upset with Joe? All that has happened and ..."

Bonita looked down at her clasped hands in her lap and changed her expression to sorrow before looking up. "It has been a bad time, but I know Joe and I know his heart. We cannot go back and change this. We still live and we must go on."

"Okay, then," Cora said, standing. "The Chief said he would not be available this morning but would try and call you later if you needed him. I'll get out of your way so you can get back to packing. I know it's a big job."

"Ah, yes. I take many breaks," Bonita said with a chuckle.

"I wish you the best, Bonita," Cora said as she stepped out onto the porch. "You can always come back to Spicetown if you decide you don't like the big city."

"Thank you, Mayor. You and Chief Harris have been very caring, and I appreciate it."

"Bye now." Cora walked to her car, uncomfortable even to turn her back on Bonita and breathed a sigh of relief once she was inside with the door shut.

Waving as she pulled her car away from the curb, Cora drove down a few blocks and turned the corner to park her car on the side of the street. Tapping the phone number for the police department, she looked in her rearview mirror.

"Spicetown PD. Can I help you?"

"Georgie, it's Cora Mae. Is the Chief in?"

"No, Mayor. He's not here at the moment. Do you want me to ask him to call?"

"I need you to get him a message, yes. I hate to interrupt him but it's rather urgent."

"I'll let him know, Mayor."

"Thank you."

Pulling back on the road, Cora continued to look in her mirrors. A white truck had been following her before she pulled over to call, yet they never drove past.

§

"You don't need to show it to me," Conrad said, holding up his hand. "I don't want to pry into union business any more than I have to. Just take a look at the purchase log from February to now and I'll ask you some questions about it."

"Okay, Chief." Parnell sat at his desk in his office typing into his laptop and Conrad was seated across from him in the visitor's chair.

"Do you see any purchases made from individuals during this time?"

"I do." Parnell glanced up in hesitation. "Do you want me to write them down?"

"No. Let me just ask questions that you can answer from what you're looking at for right now. I'm trying to minimize your trouble with Malinda later." There were also defense attorneys who liked to allege police coercion and Conrad wanted to keep this interview a simple exchange of questions and answers.

Parnell smiled. "It's okay, Chief. I'm prepared for the challenge."

"No reason to make waves when there's no water," Conrad said. "Does your purchase log reflect any union member names?"

"It does."

"Is Owen Hollingsworth's name on your list?"

"No."

"Is Joe Barney's name on your list?"

"No."

"Hmm, is Alan Avery's name on your list?"

"The site supervisor?" Parnell's eyes widened. "No, he's never sold us any tools."

"He used to be a union member, didn't he?"

"No," Parnell said, shaking his head. "He was a carpenter before he got the job with this contractor, but he was never union."

"Oh, I just assumed..."

"Nope."

"Did you like Alan Avery? What did you think of him?"

"He seemed like a decent guy," Parnell said, shrugging. "He was fair. He had it bad for Owen though. Owen got under his skin."

"That happens sometimes. Back to your list, are any of the individuals listed there current union members?"

"Yes."

"We could be here all day," Conrad said, grasping his ankle that was perched on top of his knee and chuckling. "Are any of these members currently assigned to work on the Spicetown Community Center?" Conrad patted his shirt pocket for the list he put somewhere and pulled it out. "Joshua Finley?"

Parnell shook his head from side to side.

"Max Alvarez?"

"No," Parnell said just as Conrad's phone vibrated with a text.

"Cyrus McDaniels?" Sliding his phone out of his pocket, he glanced at the display asking him to call Cora. It was urgent.

"We have a winner," Parnell said with a chuckle. "Cy sold us a combination vise and a steel roll groover."

"I don't even know what those are," Conrad said with a smile. "I need to make a quick call. I apologize, but I'll be just a minute." Holding up one finger, Conrad slipped out into the hallway and dialed Cora's cell phone.

"Connie! I'm so glad you called. I know where the tools are, the stolen tools. They're at Bonita's house. I saw the dovetail saw and a bunch of other stuff in a box."

"Cora, those may be Owen's tools. What makes you think they're—"

"Because there's a pipe bender in the box, too. I looked that up when it got stolen and that thing costs thousands. A carpenter wouldn't have a plumber's tool that cost that much."

"You've got a point. Where are you?"

"I'm driving around town. I have a white truck that's been following me since I left Bonita's and I don't want to take it home with me."

"Cora, drive to the station right now. Do not go home."

"I had just decided I was going to do that since it's still there."

"Can you tell who it is?" Conrad covered his mouth and the receiver to stifle his urge to yell at her.

"No, it gets really close to me and when I look in the mirror, it falls back."

"Go to the station now!"

"I'm headed that way," Cora said dismissively. "The reason I called is that Bonita is packing. She's going to Atlanta with Joe Barney."

"What? Does she know Joe's in jail?" Conrad wiped his forehead in exasperation.

"She does now. Where are you? Am I interrupting something?"

"I'm at the union office. Where are you?"

"Pulling into the station." Cora huffed.

"Pull in close to the cameras," Conrad instructed.

"Listen, the other thing is Bonita said Joe got in a fight with Owen and he fell to his death. He told Bonita it was an accident and he felt badly about it. She accepts that explanation and plans to move away with him. None of that makes sense to me, but she's over there furiously packing. I'm sure they are leaving town as soon as Joe gets released."

"Stay at the station and get somebody started writing a report on all of this, and I'll be back as soon as I can."

"Oh, did you find out anything at the union office?"

"Cy McDaniels." Conrad looked up and saw Malinda Grimes pointing a gun at him from the other end of the hallway.

"Hang up the phone, Chief." Malinda took a few steps closer and Conrad heard Cora was speaking as he raised his hands. "Are you breaking into my establishment? I don't believe I gave you permission to enter this building."

"Ms. Grimes, I'd appreciate it if you'd put the gun down, please. I have Mr. Dooley's consent to be here. He is in his office." Conrad tried to point while keeping his arms up, but hoped he was speaking loud enough for Cora to hear him.

"Turn around and give me your phone." Malinda took Conrad's phone from his hand and disconnected the call. Pushing the barrel of the gun into Conrad's back she said, "Walk".

"Are you planning to shoot me in the back, Ms. Grimes?"

"No Chief. I'm planning to remove you from my office."

"You can just ask me to leave and I'm happy to oblige." Conrad glanced over his shoulder and Malinda jabbed him again.

"Get out, Chief."

"Yes, ma'am. May I have my phone?" Conrad pushed the glass front door open and Malinda Grimes threw his phone out on the gravel parking lot. As soon as the door closed, Malinda turned the deadbolt. Conrad felt sorry for Parnell Dooley.

CHAPTER 32

"Conrad! Are you okay?" Cora answered the phone in a frenzy, but he could hear the dispatch radio in the background, so she was inside the police station now.

"Yeah, I'm fine. Just got thrown out of the labor union office, but it's okay. I got the info I needed—"

"Georgie, he's okay. He's in his car and on his way back," Cora yelled to dispatch. "I ran inside and told them you were being held at gunpoint at the union office and Georgie had sent a car. Did I hear that right? Were they trying to shoot you?"

"Malinda Grimes had a gun. I don't know if she meant to shoot me or not, but I left without an argument. Who was Georgie sending?"

"I don't know. I just heard her put out something over the radio."

"Well, if it was Asher, I would be a goner. I just wondered." Conrad chuckled.

"Connie! Why did you say Cyrus McDaniels when we were on the phone? Was he there? I thought maybe he had a gun."

"No, Cy is the one selling stolen tools to the union. He's connected to the thefts."

"He might be the person following me," Cora said running her hands through her hair. "I thought it might be him, but I couldn't be sure, and I couldn't understand why he would."

"If he saw you leave Bonita's, he might think you know something. I just pulled up. I'll be inside in a minute."

"Okay," Cora said and disconnected the call as she glanced up at the monitors mounted in the corner of the dispatch booth. Georgia Marks was handling a phone call and she saw Conrad get out of his car. Officer Roy Asher pulled up and parked beside him. As they walked to the side door nearest Conrad's office, Cora saw a white truck drive by in the background.

Conrad walked out to dispatch and pointed a finger at Cora, "Make yourself comfortable here because I don't want you to go home right now. Not until we secure a few things."

Cora Mae nodded solemnly.

"Tabor, I need you to bring Joe Barney back up here and put him in Interview Room 1. Then I need you to run Malinda Grimes and Cyrus McDaniels. I need whatever info you can find."

"Okay, Chief," Tabor said as he spun on his heel to retrieve Joe Barney.

"Asher, I need for you to set up the camera in Interview Room 4 and then go pick up Bonita Hollingsworth at her home. Tell her I need to talk with her and I'm short on time, so I'd appreciate her coming to the office. If she's cooperative, put her in Interview Room 4."

"Gotcha, Chief."

"Keep your eyes open because Cy McDaniels may be prowling around out there and he won't want us talking to her."

Asher gave a thumbs up sign and turned to walk back down the hallway.

"Georgie, who else is scheduled today?"

"Jennings is out on patrol." Georgie leaned out the opening of the dispatch cubicle.

"If he's free, have him run out and bring in Alan Avery. I asked him to stop by, but he hasn't been in yet. We can put him in Interview Room 3."

"Okay, Chief."

Cora Mae timidly raised her hand and Conrad smirked. "What?"

"I'm not certain, but I think the white truck pulled through the parking lot just as you and Roy walked in the office. I could go out and drive around some—"

"No." Conrad barked. "You will stay here. Briscoe, come." Snatching the leash from the hook by the dispatch door, Briscoe leaped out of the dispatch cubicle and Cora could hear the clicking of his toenails on the tile flooring as he followed Conrad down the hallway and out the side door.

Cora sighed audibly. "Oh well, can I order us some lunch, Georgie?"

Georgia Marks laughed. "Sure, Mayor. Just better make it delivery."

§

Briscoe jumped in the front seat and Conrad got them both strapped in. He needed to clear his head and think on things, so he backed out of the parking lot.

"We're going to take a cruise through town and see if we spot a white pickup. Some lunatic is chasing

Cora Mae." Conrad put his hand on Briscoe's back and patted him as he panted in excitement.

"I need to think through this mess. If Barney killed Owen, how did Cyrus get involved in selling the tools to the union? If Cy was stealing tools, then why was Barney the one at the construction site at four o'clock this morning? If it wasn't to steal tools, then why was he there?"

Conrad glanced over at Briscoe, but Briscoe was studying the landscape and not listening at all.

"Look," Conrad said, pointing. "A white truck parked at the construction site on a Saturday. Now why would that be? Huh?" Conrad hurried down Fennel Street and pulled up beside the truck, but there was no one inside.

"Let's go take a walk around. I'm sure you need to go out anyway." After stepping out of the car, Conrad motioned for Briscoe to step over and he unclipped his restraint. Grasping the leash, he stepped back and let Briscoe jump down. "Let's look around, boy."

Conrad peered down each side of the building as they strolled across the front and didn't see anyone outside. Pulling open the plywood door, Conrad led Briscoe up the stairs. "Seek"

Briscoe ran in each room of the second-floor offices and returned to Conrad with a blank stare. There was no one there. "Let's go, buddy."

As Conrad descended the staircase, he heard the sound of a motor starting and by the time they got out of the building, the white truck was gone.

The lock on the job site tool storage box was swinging open on the latch.

"We missed him, buddy. Let's go." Briscoe hopped back in the car and Conrad drove back down Fennel Street. The new flower shop was trying to raise a sign up with a pulley, but he couldn't read the front of it.

Inside the building, he could see several people bustling around. Before going back to the office, he turned on Tarragon Street and drove down near the Hollingsworth home.

Officer Asher's car was parked in front and he was on the porch talking with Bonita Hollingsworth. The discussion was animated but didn't seem aggressive. A white truck had pulled up behind Asher's squad car with the brake lights on, so the car was still in drive. Pulling up close behind him to pin him in, Conrad threw the car in park and unclipped Briscoe's restraint. "Come."

"Hey there, Cy. How are you?" Conrad strolled up to Cyrus McDaniel's driver's side door and smiled. "Join us."

"Uh, no, Chief. I'm not staying. I was—"

"Sure, you can. Step out."

"I was just going to check on Ms. Bonita and see how she was. She's busy now, so I—"

"Nonsense," Conrad said, pulling the truck door open. "Turn the truck off. Step out."

Cy stared at Conrad and then Briscoe nervously. "Uh, who's your buddy there?"

"This is Officer Briscoe."

"Oh, he's an officer, huh?"

"He is," Conrad said with his hand on his belt. "A trained police dog."

Cyrus stepped out slowly, watching Briscoe closely. "Is he going to bite me?"

"Not without reason. Can you turn around and face the vehicle, please? Hands on the vehicle."

"Uh," Cy turned but looked over his shoulder. "What's going on, Chief? Did I do something?"

"I don't know. Did you?"

"No. I didn't do nothin'."

"Do you have any weapons on you?"

"No, Chief. No, I ain't got nothin'."

"Do you care if I look in the vehicle?" Conrad patted Cy's pockets and legs.

"Why would you do that?"

"Do you give your consent for me to search your vehicle?"

"Uh, no. I don't. What's goin' on here?"

"Cross your hands behind your back," Conrad said, holding Cy's elbow to guide him as he fastened his handcuffs. "I'm detaining you for questioning." Spinning Cyrus around, Conrad glanced in the truck window. "Do you have your keys in your pocket?"

"They're in the ignition."

"Let's get them out so we can lock up your truck. It should be okay parked here for a little while." Conrad pulled open the truck door and reached for the keys as he glanced in the floorboard of the passenger side seat and heard Briscoe growl. "Are you kicking at Officer Briscoe?"

"He's growling at me," Cy said angrily. "Did you bring him just so he could attack me?"

"No, actually I brought him along because I thought he needed to take a leak." Conrad smiled as Briscoe took a couple of steps toward Cyrus and lifted his leg on his shoe.

Cyrus yelled and jumped from foot to foot as if his feet were on fire.

"Oh, settle down," Conrad said as he laughed. Briscoe learned that trick while they were bored in Kentucky and Conrad had been forced to walk him morning and night down the concrete sidewalks. It had been a useful trick to get Briscoe to go on demand, but he had never imagined it would be this amusing. "Let's go."

CHAPTER 33

Conrad shoved Cyrus McDaniels into Interview Room 2. "Have a seat. I'll be with you shortly."

Slamming the door, Conrad looked around for Tabor. "Barney in number one?"

"Yeah, Chief. Jennings is on his way in with Avery." Tabor held out the papers in his hands. "This is what I got."

"Chief, Asher is en route," Georgia said as she twirled her chair around to grab the phone.

Conrad nodded and looked at the printouts that Tabor provided. He pulled his reading glasses from his pocket and read through the information on Cyrus McDaniels and then the report Tabor had completed on Cora Mae's visit to Bonita.

"So, you think Barney and Bonita are together?" Conrad said to Cora as she looked up from her seat at an empty desk. "I mean before Owen died. Do you think—?"

"I would have never believed it before today, but yes, it looks like it might have been that way. That may have been why they fought."

"Hmm," Conrad hummed as he stroked his chin. "This changes things. I can't believe she shared this."

"I don't think she knows about the tools or the union issues. I think she's in a much smaller, simpler world than we are, and she doesn't see anything wrong with what happened."

"Naive and insecure." Conrad nodded.

"Chief," Georgia hollered from the dispatch booth. "Asher just pulled up with the wife and Jennings is five minutes out."

"Now that you will soon have half the town here, do you suppose I could go home?" Cora smiled smugly.

"Aw, I guess so," Conrad said with a smile.

"I've got a roast in the crockpot. If you get done here by seven o'clock, come by and get some dinner," Cora said, standing up to reach for her purse.

"Oh, I'll be done by then," Conrad said with a confident smile. "See you later."

"Chief, do you want me to call Wink in early so he can help you interview?" Tabor leaned against the dispatch entrance. "Or I can help if you'd like."

"Nah, Wink's off today and I don't want to disturb him. I don't really think this will take all that long. I'm going to start with Barney."

Conrad waved as Cora went out the front door and turned to go into Interview Room 1.

"Wink will be sore that he missed out on this," Eugene Tabor said to Georgia Marks. "That's why he likes working nights. He thinks nothing happens in the daytime."

"I think he's got a big date tonight," Georgia whispered. "He's seeing Mitzi Boyle that works down at Louise's Beauty Shop. She got mad with him last week when he kept getting called out to work. I think if he left her tonight, she'd be done with him."

"I bet if I called him, he'd be here."

"Probably, but she'll have to learn that later, because you're not calling him today," Georgia said, pointing a scolding finger at Tabor as he laughed.

§

"Perfect timing! I was just getting ready to spoon it up." Cora held open her front door for Conrad. "Come on in."

"It smells good in here."

Cora scurried down the hallway when she heard a bell ding. "The rolls are done."

"I'll make the drinks," Conrad said as he opened the cabinet door. He had watched Cora wait on him enough times that he knew where most things were kept.

"Tell me what happened," Cora said as she snapped the oven door shut. "Did you lock everyone up?"

"No, just Cyrus for right now. He had stolen items in his truck." Conrad had sent Asher back to Bonita's house to take photographs of the tools in the floorboard of Cyrus's truck. Alan Avery confirmed the items were removed from the construction site toolbox and filed a report.

"So, he was the thief!" Cora buttered the tops of the rolls and reached in the cabinet for a serving platter.

"Yeah, he lifted a saw from the construction site today and Briscoe lifted a leg on his foot in return." Conrad's laughter roared when Cora gasped.

"He didn't. Did Briscoe pee on him?" Cora smiled guiltily.

"He did indeed," Conrad said. "I taught him that little trick in Kentucky."

"You told Briscoe to pee on Cyrus?" Cora shook her head. "Shame on you, Connie."

The scolding just made Conrad laugh louder.

"Did you find out what's going on with Bonita and Joe? Were they having an affair?"

"It appears so," Conrad said as he carried the glasses to the table. "Bonita is quite taken with Barney, but I get a vibe that Barney is just hanging in there for the insurance money."

"Oh, no."

"Yeah," Conrad said, opening the cabinet door for plates. "Alan Avery gave Barney a key to the tools so he could clean up after Owen. Alan thought Owen was leaving tools out intentionally so he could come back later and steal them, so he thought Barney would want to help Owen out. Alan asked him to clean up behind Owen. It would keep Owen out of trouble and Alan wouldn't lose tools. Win-win, except it wasn't. Barney didn't care about Owen and he took a couple of the tools himself, knowing Owen would get blamed. Those tools you saw at Bonita's house are stolen, but Barney is going to return them. I don't think the judge will do anything Monday on the trespass charge and if he returns the tools, Alan doesn't want to press charges on the theft."

"And why was he at the construction site early Saturday morning?" Cora sat a bowl of mixed vegetables on the table and walked back to the counter for the roast platter.

"He said he was supposed to meet Cyrus there, but I guess we showed up and scared Cyrus off. Barney had figured out that Cyrus was stealing, and since he was leaving town, he offered to sell his toolbox keys to him. He didn't need them anymore."

"Pretty low," Cora said, frowning. "Anything for money. Joe doesn't care who he hurts with his actions. Those thefts affect the success of the community center and cost his union a lot of money."

"He's not a stellar human being, but it's not illegal to be a dirt bag."

"Bonita didn't want Owen dead, did she?" Cora placed napkins on the table and waved Conrad over to sit down.

"I don't think so. I think that really was an accident. He fell when they were fighting upstairs."

"But why were they both there that Friday night? Why is everybody always going to the construction site after hours?" Cora's hands flew open in frustration.

"After Owen talked with Alan Avery and left that Friday night, we think he drove back by and saw Barney's truck there, so he went to see what he was doing. Maybe he was looking for him. We don't know. We do know Owen had found out that Joe visited his house one evening when he was at the demolition derby and he confronted Joe about Bonita. Joe was actually there to steal something, but he said Owen just tore into him. Took a swing at him. He never asked him why he was there. As far as he knows, Owen had no clue about the tool thefts." Conrad sliced open a roll and buttered it liberally as Cora's cat, Marmalade, rubbed her head against his ankles.

"Maybe Owen had just been told about the affair. To show up and act that quickly, it sounds like he was operating on pure emotion," Cora said.

"Joe got all tangled up when he freaked out and tried to cover everything up. He drove Owen's truck out of town to hide it and then didn't know how to get back to his own. It wasn't the best plan, and I imagine he did panic. To me, that says it wasn't planned."

"Mercy," Cora said, taking a sip of her iced tea. "What did you do with the lady who held a gun on you at the union?"

"Oh, the union," Conrad said with a chuckle. "Turns out they are a bunch of thieves, too. Monday I'm going to see about a subpoena for their records, but I'd not be surprised if Malinda Grimes has already shredded them."

"What are you going to do if the records are gone?"

"I've got enough testimony from the workers to bring charges, and I think the insurance company will join right in. Parnell Dooley isn't dirty. He knew something wasn't right, but I think he felt powerless to correct it. I don't know if the union will support him or not. That remains to be seen and will be telling in and of itself."

"The woman with the gun is the one? She was filing false insurance claims?" Cora held out her plate for Conrad to spoon her some potatoes.

"Malinda Grimes. She's from the regional union office, not this local chapter. She paid Cyrus McDaniels for the stolen tools, but he only got a small fraction of what the insurance company paid. Then she doctored the financial records to show the insurance payment returned, the tool recovered, and listed Cyrus's payment as being for something other than what she bought."

"A crafty girl!"

"Whew! It's going to be quite a mess to straighten out, but I suspect the insurance company has experts at that. I'm just filing conspiracy to commit burglary and trespass charges on her because she enlisted Cyrus to steal. I can do that on Cy's and Parnell's statement. Then I'll just stand back and turn the lawyers loose."

§

"I'm so proud of you." Mitzi cooed as she snuggled against Wink on the couch. "We had a wonderful dinner and you've been so attentive tonight. I haven't seen you look at your phone one time."

"It's possible to do," Wink said as he kissed the top of her head. "Just not all the time. Sometimes I just have to go at unexpected times. That's my job."

Mitzi pushed her bottom lip out in a pouting frown. "I just don't know if I can take being stood up or walked out on again. It's not right. No job should control your life that way. Everyone deserves some time of their own."

"I got lots of that," Wink said, hugging her closer. "I just can't always keep promises. When something happens, I have to go."

"Well, I'm happy that nothing happened in Spicetown today." Mitzi smiled and reached up to stroke Wink's cheek.

"Me too, babe."

∞

★ The Spicetown Star ★

~GRAND OPENING~

Spicetown Welcome Center

The Spicetown Welcome Center and Community Center will open to the public on Friday, October 4th at 7:00 p.m. The public is welcome to come tour the building. Refreshments will be provided.

The newly renovated factory will now be equipped to offer the Spicetown community a gathering spot for town events, plays, musicals and celebrations. The space can also be rented for local events and registration is available on the Spicetown City Hall website.

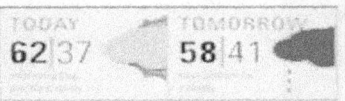

TODAY 62 | 37   TOMORROW 58 | 41

Chicken Pot Pie Soup

1/4 cup unsalted butter
2-3 cups chopped cooked chicken
1 teaspoon minced garlic
1/4 cup all-purpose flour
3 cups chicken stock
1 cup chopped potato
1 teaspoon chopped fresh thyme
1/2 teaspoon poultry seasoning or Italian seasoning
2 cups milk
1/2 cup frozen (thawed) peas and carrots
2 tablespoons chopped fresh parsley
1/2 teaspoon ground black pepper and 1/2 tsp. salt
Add vegetables you enjoy: celery, carrots, corn, green beans, mushrooms, peppers, etc.

1. Melt butter over medium to low heat until it is foaming.
2. Add hard veggies (celery, carrots, mushrooms, peppers and onion if you want).
3. Increase heat to medium and cook until vegetables are tender and translucent, about 5 minutes.
4. Add garlic; cook for 1 minute.
5. Add flour; cook, stirring constantly, until mixture is blond color, about 3 minutes.
6. Whisk in broth, and add potato, thyme and poultry seasoning.
7. Increase heat and stir frequently.
8. Then reduce heat and simmer, uncovered, until vegetables are tender, and soup is slightly thickened, about 30 minutes.
9. Remove from heat. Stir in milk. Add cooked chicken and soft veggies (peas, corn, etc.), if you like.

Next in The Spicetown Mystery Series
A Tough Nut to Crack

I'd love to hear from you!

Find me on Facebook, Goodreads, Twitter, my website or join my email list for upcoming news!
www.SheriRichey.com

www.ingramcontent.com/pod-product-compliance
Lightning Source LLC
Chambersburg PA
CBHW022302210725
29900CB00044BC/618